One True Love

Also by Lori Copeland

Belles of Timber Creek Series

TWICE LOVED
THREE TIMES BLESSED

One True Love

Belles of Timber Creek

Lori Copeland

AVON
INSPIRE
An Imprint of HarperCollins*Publishers*

This book is a work of fiction. The characters, incidents, and dialogue are drawn from the author's imagination and are not to be construed as real. Any resemblance to actual events or persons, living or dead, is entirely coincidental.

ISBN-13: 978-1-61664-169-6

In loving memory of:

Carolyn Sue Smart, a beloved sister-in-law who
went to be with the Lord on June 19, 2008.
You fought a good fight, sweetie, and I
know that today you're walking hand in
hand with Dan, both in the presence of
the Lord. Wait for me at the Gate.

Cheryl Sue (Buxton) Tapp, loving grandmother,
mother, and wife who took her heavenly flight
on July 14, 2008. You've left a legacy of love
and caring to your grandchildren, daughters,
and family. The Copelands are blessed by your
daughter, Shelley, and our granddaughter, Audrey.
Maws, you will be missed, but never forgotten.

Trust God from the bottom of your heart;
Don't try to figure out everything on your own.
Listen for God's voice in everything you do . . .
Proverbs 3:5–6 *(The Message)*

Chapter 1

Copper Wilson erased the blackboard in the Beeder's Cove schoolhouse and imagined that she was wiping clean all the negative memories and consequences of the past few months of her life. Months that had been filled with more war and rain than she had ever imagined possible, and she was ready to leave both behind.

She heard the door open and turned to see Benjamin Fowler enter the room. Swiftly removing his hat, the school board member smiled. "Good morning, Miss Wilson."

Copper returned the greeting. "And a beautiful morning it is." Though not so welcome for her best friend, Willow Gray. Noon yesterday the bank had auctioned off her uncle's home, a place that had given Willow, Audrey, and Copper shelter after they had arrived from Timber Creek. Copper worked to put the worrisome sale aside and focus on the future, but Willow's quandary had been in the back of her mind since she opened her eyes that morning.

Mr. Fowler briskly rubbed his hands together. "I thought I would come by and check on the stove. Evenings are getting a mite frosty lately."

"How thoughtful of you. I notice we have a sufficient stack of dry wood. Please extend my thanks to the person responsible." Last week had been Copper's first on the job, and the adjustment had proven difficult. She had tried to start a fire after school one afternoon just to be sure the stove worked properly. The old relic had smoked, and the damp wood smoldered more than it had burned.

Finding dry wood had been difficult for the townspeople. Copper knew the children could wear their coats and mittens inside the classroom if necessary, but that was no way to start a school year. She suspected the old pipe might have gotten clogged over the summer, perhaps by some bird's nest-building activity.

Fowler nodded. "That would be Henry Franks. We didn't get the heavy rains that plagued Thunder Ridge, but we got enough to make most of our firewood wet."

Wet. Mr. Fowler didn't know the meaning of the word. Copper's thoughts turned to all those weeks she'd spent in Thunder Ridge with her two best friends, Willow and Audrey; of standing puddles, drenched clothing, and leaky roofs she had dealt with in Judge Madison's old house. It had rained solidly for weeks. And yesterday, because of bank foreclosure, the old house had been auctioned off. Frankly, though it broke her heart to think of Willow losing her uncle's house, the loss might be more blessing than curse. Now that Willow had married Thunder Ridge's handsome sawmill owner, Tucker Gray, life might be easier for the young couple if they moved into his one-room cabin. Then when babies started to arrive Tucker could add rooms with the help of his cousins, Eli and Caleb.

She limped to the stove sitting in the corner of the room, a large black atrocity that looked capable of warming Hades had it been in good repair. The way it had smoked last week caused her to wonder about the history of the potbellied monster. The top hinge on the door was crooked and seemed weak. The left front leg was missing and had been replaced by an uneven block of wood. The pipe had a definite slant to it because the stove had not been placed directly underneath the hole that went through the roof.

It seemed a little unsafe, and she had mentioned it to Mr. Fowler on her way to work this morning. Mr. Fowler focused on her limp. "Did you suffer an accident over the weekend?"

Copper glanced at the injured foot and shrugged. "Actually I injured the ankle a few weeks ago and it hasn't fully healed. These chilly mornings seem to aggravate the condition."

"How'd you hurt it?"

"It's a long story."

"I'm in no hurry."

But she was. The children would arrive shortly. Yet he was her employer. "My friend Audrey and I were carrying ice one night to help break a friend's high fever. Willow had received a blow to the head that left her unconscious for days. She almost died." Sadness washed over Copper when she thought how close she'd come to losing her best friend. "Those were dark times. We thought she might not survive the injury, but our prayers were answered."

"I trust she's doing well now?"

"Very well." She smiled. "She married Tucker Gray this past Saturday."

"Ah yes. Tucker. Good man, as are his cousins, Eli and Caleb. We do business with the mill." Thunder Ridge and Beeder's Cove were a short distance apart.

She bent to carefully place wood into the stove. "They are indeed fine men."

Fowler took a step back and his gaze followed the stovepipe to where it jutted through the roof. "Better let me climb up there and take another look before we light a fire. The building sat empty since the war started, and someone was supposed to clean the flue, but it's very possible a bird or two has built a nest up there again. I'll go take a quick peek."

She nodded. "Be careful."

When the front door closed, she absently stacked dry branches around logs in the stove, thinking about all she had to do before the children arrived. Automatically she reached for a match. Then she remembered Mr. Fowler. He was on the roof, peering down the chimney. She tried to stomp out the small blaze but quickly withdrew her good foot. The tinder had a good hold. She glanced overhead, noting the sound of footsteps. By the time the wood ignited Fowler would be on his way down. In seconds the dry tinder blazed. Glancing at her timepiece locket, she quickly rose and hobbled to her desk. Children would be arriving soon and she had not yet registered their last test scores.

A dull ache settled around the rim of her shoe and she winced. The ankle was truly acting up today. Must be a coming change in weather.

Fowler opened the front door and stuck his head in, all

smiles. "I believe we're in business. The stove seems to be drawing fine."

Copper glanced up from the recording ledger. "Thank you, Mr. Fowler. The room is starting to warm nicely."

"Anything else I can do?"

"Can't think of anything. Thank you."

"Sure am glad to have you, Miss Wilson. It's nice to have school open again." With a tip of his hat, he closed the door.

Precisely at eight-thirty, Copper rang the large brass bell that hung on the outside wall above the small porch. The sound carried to the entire community, signaling that class was about to begin. She had thirteen pupils, ranging from six to fifteen years of age. The two youngest, Emily and Mackey, belonged to the Matthews family. Their grandfather was reportedly the wealthiest man around. The children wore clothes far superior to those of the others. Most of her little flock came from various parts of the district and were poor as church mice. She dropped the cord and took her stance at the front door.

"Good morning, Miss Wilson."

"Good morning, Suzanne. Edward."

And so it went as the children filed by swinging their dinner pails. Coats were hung on the pegs in the short hallway and dinner pails stored beneath the desks. By eight forty-five class was in session. The two youngest Matthewses sat in the front row, fidgeting.

"Today," Copper began, "we're going to talk about American history and the Revolutionary War."

She picked up her ruler. "Now. Warren Brown." She knew full well the younger children needed to settle down before she addressed their study, but she had already noted that

Warren had a tendency to forget his homework assignments, and she thought he might improve if she made his lack of responsibility obvious to the other students. "One of the most famous quotations from the Revolutionary War period is, 'I only regret that I have but one life to lose for my country.' The words, spoken as British authorities executed him for spying, were spoken by whom?"

Something in the stove made a loud *pop*, and in the silence it brought a startled sound from little Emily. Someone else giggled.

Copper glanced at the stove and then scowled at the giggler. Silence returned. "You have all heard sounds like that from a stove. Now settle down.

"Now, was the quote spoken by Benedict Arnold, Patrick Henry, Nathan Hale, or Paul Revere?"

She had just posed the question to Warren when a loud crash turned everyone's attention toward the front door. Before Copper could even form a thought concerning the cause of the racket, a large yellow tomcat streaked down the aisle toward her, followed by two large hound dogs, both barking at the tops of their lungs. Evidently the front door had been left slightly ajar and the cat dashed through. With typical canine enthusiasm the dogs had slammed into the door and continued the chase into the classroom.

The cat, openly desperate to find a perch above the yapping jaws, jumped onto the stove but immediately leaped back to the floor on the other side. Skidding to a halt, the lead dog slammed into the stove and knocked it off the block of wood. The stove tipped over, causing the door to fly open.

Reversing direction, the feline headed back toward the door. This time it jumped up and dug its claws into a jacket hanging from a peg, and then climbed up onto a shelf running the length of the coatrack above the pegs.

The episode took only scant seconds and Copper hadn't had time to comprehend any of it when someone cried out, "The floor's on fire."

She whirled to look and was immediately grabbed by an inexpressible terror. A schoolteacher's greatest fear is a burning schoolhouse with the children still inside, and this was exactly what she was facing. To make matters worse, the doorway out of the building was blocked by the warring animals.

Instinctively the children flocked to her, and without instruction they moved in a huddle to the side of the room opposite the stove. The pipe that had been dangling from the roof fell with a loud bang, and soot flew out to mix with the smoke. With incredible speed the fire expanded in a semicircle along the floor.

A child started to cry, and then another joined in. Copper knelt down and wrapped her arms around the weeping ones. "It's going to be all right," she cooed, hoping that she sounded more confident than she felt.

She scanned the windows on the clear side of the building with the idea of maybe escaping through one of them. "Harold," she said to the fifteen-year-old, "try to open a window. Hurry."

He tried the closest one, then another, and then a third. None would budge.

"Never mind," she shouted. "See if you can do anything with that cat so the dogs will clear the doorway."

Harold moved to the back of the room where the age-old battle between cat and canine was still in full progress.

When he got close to the nearest hound it turned and bared its teeth and growled at the boy. He hesitated and looked back at Copper, clearly undecided about what to do next.

"Grab the cat and put it out the door," Copper yelled. *"Now!"*

Plunging into the fray, he reached up on the shelf and tried to snatch the cat. It immediately scratched him several times, and Copper had a fleeting thought that the tabby might jump on his head. He leaped back and glanced at Copper.

She assessed the fire's movement along the floor. It had almost reached the front-row seats and looked as if it might soon start to climb up the wall. Suddenly she had an idea. "Harold, put on some gloves and seize that cat."

Harold took a pair of gloves from the nearest jacket, snatched the cat, ran over to the door, and threw it outside. The dogs nearly knocked him down as they rushed through the doorway.

By now smoke enveloped the room.

"Children, quickly, everybody outside." Copper urged the traumatized children to hurry, without causing them to panic. It seemed an eternity before they reached the door and exited into the clear air.

"Keep moving. Don't stop. Get away from the building," she shouted. When she felt they were safe she turned and looked back. By now smoke was boiling out of the front door. She counted the children. Ten, eleven, twe— *Count again.* Ten, eleven . . . A thought more horrific than death struck her. There were two children missing.

She turned to Harold. "Harold, count the children. How many are here?"

Confusion, then comprehension, flashed across the boy's face. He reached out and touched each head as he counted. "There are only eleven, Miss Copper."

No, dear God. Please no. Please.

Whirling, Copper ran back up the steps onto the porch and through the door. The smoke was so thick she couldn't see more than two feet in front of her. Coughing, she raised an arm to her eyes as they began to water. As she moved past the hanging coats she stumbled over something. Reaching down, she encountered a handful of curly hair. She knelt and reached out to grab the child, and her hand hit another small neck. Both of them! They were huddled together on the floor. How had she reached the outside without them? Which two were they? It didn't matter! She had them both.

All three were coughing and gagging as she crawled toward the door, dragging the children with her. *Don't let go of either one of them*, flashed over and over in her mind. *You'll never find them again.*

It seemed an eternity, but it was actually only minutes before they reached the porch. She tried to get the children to stand up and go down the steps ahead of her. As she started to take the first step down she fell against the railing and it collapsed. The last thing she remembered was a fiery pain shooting through her ankle into her leg and then the sensation of falling.

Chapter 2

Gasping, Copper sat upright when cold water hit her face. Pairs of expectant eyes formed a circle above her.

"Sorry to startle you, Miss Wilson, but you passed out." Harold's wary expression looked as if he thought he'd be taken to the woodshed for the hostile act. Black smoke pillared skyward, and folks came running. Benjamin Fowler was first on the scene, shouting orders to stay back. A bucket brigade formed and men and women rushed back and forth from the school well and the river to try to save the burning building. The timber went up like dry chaff; nothing could be done other than to stand back and watch the demolition.

Harold helped Copper to her feet and she collapsed against the boy. "I can't stand, Harold. I've injured my ankle again."

Overhearing, Fowler ordered Harold to carry the new schoolmarm to her room at the Widow Potts's. Anxious parents gathered children into wagons to cart home.

Mr. Matthews stepped forward to speak a word to Copper, who was leaning heavily on Harold's arm. The fifteen-year-old was a strapping kid, bigger than most men and reportedly able to more than hold his own when working with the men.

Howard Matthews's expression reflected his deep gratitude. Copper had already heard that Howard's devotion to his grandchildren was legendary. "Miss Wilson, my grandchildren tell me that you went back into that burning building to rescue them."

She brushed his praise aside. "It was nothing. I didn't know until now which two children it was. I just thank God I was able to find Emily and Mackey in time."

"It may be a small sacrifice for you, but it means the world to me. Those children . . ." He bit his quivering lower lip. "You have my deepest gratitude."

Copper wanted to comfort him, but the white-hot pain radiating from her ankle rendered her speechless.

Harold nodded. "I've got to get the teacher to the Widow Potts." He scooped her up in his arms and carried her the short distance to the Potts house.

Finally she lay on her bed in the widow's house, the familiar stench of Mrs. Potts's snuff and strong scented lavender filling her nostrils. Harold quickly excused himself as if he was extremely uncomfortable in a lady's private setting.

Eloise Potts fussed about, removing Copper's boots.

"Is my ankle swollen more?" Copper asked, picturing the injury now the size of a July watermelon.

An audible gasp escaped the widow. "It's . . . oh my dear."

Sinking back to the pillow, Copper closed her eyes. The *oh my dear* answered her question.

"We must send for Dr. Smith immediately."

Poor Dr. Smith. He'd been treating the ill from the wagon train, looking after Willow, traveling back and forth from Blackberry Hill and Thunder Ridge. The poor man must be exhausted, and now he would once again be summoned to Beeder's Cove.

Copper was torn between fear, not wanting to see the injury, yet curiosity, wanting to know what it looked like. Surely it was a simple wrench—an added nuisance to the one that she'd endured the past month. "Is that necessary? It's just a sprain and it was healing nicely until I turned it again getting the children out of the schoolhouse." Another sprain wasn't going to make her swoon.

The widow sank to the side of the bed. "It is far more than a sprain, my dear. I'll send someone immediately to fetch the doctor, and get a cold compress. Meanwhile, you rest and I'll fix you a nice cup of hot tea." She disappeared, and Copper lay back on the pillow. Drats. One more delay, and delays seemed to have become the norm with her. She couldn't be off her feet long. If she'd broken a bone this time, the doctor would set it and she could get around on crutches. Teaching didn't require her to be nimble. Harold could chase down the unruly ones, and . . . An unwelcome thought occurred to her. What if the schoolhouse had burned to the ground and she was out of a job yet again?

Ever since the war ended, it had been one thing after another. Everyone thought the end of the war would mean a fresh start. But who knew fresh starts were so hard to keep?

By late afternoon the doctor arrived. Copper managed a proper apology, and the good man brushed her chagrin aside.

"You Timber Creek gals sure attract your share of trouble," he teased. "Now what's this about the ankle? I thought the injury was healing nicely."

The widow explained about the morning fire, and Copper turned the ankle.

"How bad was the fire?" Copper asked.

"Burned to the ground, I hear."

Her greatest fear realized. At least none of the children was hurt, but this would mean more delays in starting school. Copper winced when the doctor gently stretched and twisted the injured foot. His expression changed from congenial to serious. The change was not lost on Copper. It was not a good sign.

"Broken?" she guessed.

"My dear woman, in all my days I don't believe I've ever seen a bone more . . ." He closed his mouth.

Broken. That meant more weeks of hobbling around.

"No, I don't *think* the bone is broken. Not exactly—I'd venture it's severely twisted and jammed out of place. Perhaps I can snap it back . . ."

She closed her eyes and gritted her teeth. "Do what you must."

The doctor placed his left hand on her leg, about halfway to her knee. Then he gave a gentle, soft twist to her foot. Copper, barely able to stifle a scream, gave a long, slow groan. "That's very tender, isn't it?" the doctor asked. Copper could only nod, fighting off nausea.

He sighed. "I fear that I am going to do more damage."

Beads of sweat trickled down her temple. Never had she endured such pain. "What will we do? We can't leave it like this."

"No," he mused. "We most certainly can't leave it like this."

While he was making up his mind, she needed reprieve. "The pain . . . can you give me anything for this miserable pain?"

The doctor folded the sheet over her injured foot. "I have laudanum." He opened his satchel and brought out a small brown vial. "Open your mouth."

Copper obeyed, and he administered a few drops under her tongue. "This should help you rest."

"What about the foot? Does it need to be set right away?"

"Set—uh . . ." He absently patted her arm. "You rest. We'll talk later."

For once Copper didn't have the energy to argue. The radiating pain hurt like blue blazes, and all she wanted was release.

By the time the widow ushered the doctor out of the room, she was already drowsy.

Weeks of hobbling around on crutches. She sighed. An evil cloud hung over the women of Timber Creek.

A dark, oppressive fog that refused to budge.

Laudanum. Copper didn't fully understand the medicine, but she grew to love its effect. From the first dropperful the pain lifted and she floated in a blissful haze where faces and voices drifted in and out. Widow Potts had more company than any one person Copper had ever known.

Every few hours—or maybe days, Copper was never certain—hushed whispers filled her bedroom. Some voices she recognized, like Benjamin Fowler, Dr. Smith. Cold encompassed her fast.

Another time the Matthewses—Mackey and Emily's mother, father, and grandfather—were back, expressing gratitude for Copper's heroic actions.

A man's voice, Howard Matthews's, penetrated the fog. He sat beside her bed for the longest time talking. Just talking. His words floated in her mind and she knew he was speaking of how he loved his grandchildren, Emily and Mackey, how they were the reason for his existence.

With regularity the laudanum was offered, and she obediently opened her mouth and accepted the powerful respite.

In her dreams—and the drug did create the strangest dreams—Audrey came to visit. The young woman held her hand and cried a bit, but then said everything was going to be fine. This curse they were under must lift sometime.

Copper recalled smiling and saying something—she had no idea what, but as long as the medicine worked, she wasn't persuaded the curse was such a bad thing.

And then the drug's effect would lift, and she would orient to her environment—unfamiliar surroundings now. She was lying in the back of a buckboard. Caleb Gray held the reins, and Eli and Audrey sat beside him. Snow fell from a leaden sky.

Snow in October? That couldn't be right. The laudanum was nice, but soon she would have to regain her sense and have the foot set before the bone refused to knit together. The thought caused her to sit straight up.

Audrey whirled on the buckboard seat. "Lie down, Copper!"

"Audrey? What's happening?" The haze wavered, and the

alarm jarred her. This lethargic state had gone on for too long. Something was amiss . . .

Audrey climbed into the wagon bed and Copper spotted the small brown vial of elixir.

"No . . ." She pushed the dropper aside when Audrey tried to open her mouth. "Stop! What's happening to me?"

"Just lie back. You're fine. We'll have you out of the snow very soon."

"Snow? It doesn't snow in October."

"Around these parts it appears the weather can do what it wants."

Now that was a definite grumble in Audrey's voice, and Audrey rarely grumbled.

"Lie down, Copper!" The sharpness was so unlike Audrey's patient nature.

Copper lay down.

"Open your mouth."

"I don't want to . . ." She choked and spat as liquid seeped down her throat. "I *demand* to know what's going on and where you're taking me . . ."

Oh drat. Fuzzy objects were starting to take on familiar colorful edges. Caleb. Even if Audrey had taken leave of her senses, he would help her. "Caleb, please help me. Fetch me a pair of crutches so I can get up and move around . . ."

"I surely will, Copper. The moment you're ready for crutches you'll have them." He turned to look over his shoulder, and she realized she'd never seen such a grave expression on this man's features. "You have my solemn promise."

"Eli . . ." she pleaded, sinking lower and lower into the medicinal bliss.

"Rest, Copper. You'll have your crutches. I'll make them myself if need be."

"Promise?"

"You have my word."

Eli was a sterling craftsman. And he loved Audrey. The warm woolly feeling allowed her to relax. Suddenly she stirred.

"Where are the children?"

"Children?" Audrey turned to look at her.

"My class. How soon can we resume school?"

"Soon."

"They've found a new schoolroom this quickly?"

"I believe I've heard talk of using the town hall until they can rebuild."

"The town hall. It doesn't have a blackboard."

"The school board will work it out. Now you rest."

Well, she couldn't teach without a blackboard. Mr. Fowler would have to come up with something soon. Warren still had to answer the question about who said what during the Revolutionary War. At the moment she had forgotten the answer—for that matter, she'd forgotten the question. She opened her mouth to catch a fat snowflake.

Snow. In early October. How very strange even for the Texas panhandle.

Chapter 3

Hell hath no fury like a woman in pain. That wasn't Scripture, just the plain truth. And then the nightmares started.

First, Josh Redlin, the wagon master from the stricken wagon train that had been forced to stop in Thunder Ridge, appeared. Oh, she recognized *him* straightaway. His deep timbre rumbled above the other men. Vaguely she recalled his taunts.

"What is *your name, Miss . . . ?"*

He'd known her name. He just loved to aggravate her.

Around her, hushed conversations were going on, and then the voices would drift off, in a sea of pain.

Then Redlin would be back, only now he wouldn't leave. He hung around, his voice prominent above the others, bossing her around. *Lie still. Drink this. Go to sleep. Wake up.*

He wasn't her keeper. If she had the energy she'd tell him.

Then she awoke bundled like a Christmas goose in thick blankets, racing through the night in some sort of fancy carriage. The laudanum wore off long enough for her to question her surroundings, and then there was a man—an elderly man—Mackey and Emily's grandfather? This man would wrap her blanket more snugly and speak words of encouragement, of comfort.

The nightmares never let up, they just rolled like an angry sea one after the other after the other . . .

"Wagons roll!"

Roll 'em out, roll 'em out, roll 'em out . . . echoed through Copper's mind.

"Now love, you're going to be better very soon."

Copper opened her eyes to see Adele fussing over her blankets. Adele? She had been part of the wagon train that had left for Colorado more than a week ago. What was she doing here?

The medicine. Copper must be dreaming. She closed her eyes waiting for the images to fade, but they didn't. Adele sat beside her in a rocking chair, calmly knitting what looked to be baby booties. Copper's bleary gaze roamed the overhead canvas. Her body absorbed the lurch and sway—she was in a wagon. Going where? She struggled to sit up.

Adele laid her knitting aside while pushing her back to the pallet with a strong hand. "It's good to see that you're back with us."

Back from where? "Where am I?"

"Just lie still, honey. You've hurt your ankle real bad. You're on your way to Fort Riceson to see the best doctor money can buy."

Copper's first thought was she must be on the way to the poorhouse because she didn't have the money for doctors—and since when did a sprained ankle deserve such fuss? Pain radiated up her leg, and she bit her lower lip. "I don't have the money for a doctor."

"The bill is paid in full," Adele said. "You don't have nary a worry." Yet the woman's anxious countenance suggested otherwise. Adele was usually all smiles in the worst of times, and if her pinched face was any indication, these were awful times.

"The children?"

"All safe as little buggers in a tree stump. You did well, dearie. That fire could have caused a lot of grief. Why, Howard Matthews has ordered that you be treated like royalty."

"Howard Matthews?"

"Little Emily and Mackey's grandpa. Now there's a grateful man. You saved the two most precious things he has on this old earth, and he means to repay you, he does."

Slowly images returned. The fire. Screaming, terrified children. Choking black smoke.

The schoolhouse was gone. Copper closed her eyes. She thought she'd left trouble well behind when she left Thunder Ridge, but it seemed it only followed her to Beeder's Cove.

She swallowed against a dry throat. "I'm thankful there were no serious injuries."

"Except for you. You injured that ankle fiercely getting Mackey and Emily to safety."

Bit by bit it all came back. Panic. Pain. Incredible pain. "I didn't break the ankle; it was sprained and I turned it again, that's all."

"No ma'am. That's not all." Adele's eyes gentled. "Honey, you've hurt it real bad, and we're on our way to see a doctor the elder Matthews served with in the war. Seems this man can work miracles, if there's one to be had."

But the bone *wasn't* broken. That much she remembered— yet the pain the likes of which she'd experienced couldn't come from a mere sprain.

"Couldn't Dr. Smith set the bone?"

"No, the injury is far beyond his experience. Howard Matthews says no one's touching that ankle until Dale Dyson has a look-see."

"Dale Dyson?"

"The doctor that served with the elder Matthews's company before he retired from the cavalry. The doctor and his family are at the fort now." Adele reached for her needles. "Funny how Howard Matthews comes from a long line of moneyed folks, but he spent his life—or most of it—in service to his country. Some people are pure gold. You know?"

The wagon hit a rut and Copper winced. Her thoughts cleared enough to know she was with the wagon train . . .

Oh dear heavens. Josh Redlin. That *had* been his voice she'd heard.

Adele frowned. "Ah now, you're having some real pain. It's time for more medicine."

"No . . . I can't think when I take the medicine, Adele."

"And why would you be needing to think?"

"Do Willow and Audrey know about my injury?"

"Land yes. Audrey spent the past two days at your side."

"What about school? The children have missed so much because of the rains, and now this?"

"Yvonne filled in while she was gone. The young widow ain't a teacher, but she can follow Audrey's lesson plans and keep the Thunder Ridge young'uns in order. I'd imagine she welcomes the diversion what with her losing her husband so recently. Audrey returned this morning." Before Copper knew it, Adele wedged the laudanum between her dry, cracked lips.

She involuntarily swallowed. "How far to Fort Riceson?"

"Forty or so miles, but you're not to worry. I'll be with you," the older woman promised. "Won't be the same as having Willow and Audrey, but I gave my word that you'd not want for a thing. And Howard Matthews will hold my feet to the fire if I don't do my job."

So another unwelcome chapter in my life. Copper mentally sighed. More never-ending hours of living in a drugged haze. Then the ankle must be set . . . or fixed . . . or whatever this Dr. Dyson would do, then allowed to knit before she could make the long trek back. It was entirely possible that Audrey would marry Eli Gray during her absence, and Copper wouldn't be there to participate in the nuptials. Hot tears rolled from the corners of her eyes.

"Now now, lovey." Adele patted her arm. "You're blessed to have such good care. Don't be borrowing trouble when you don't want to have to pay it back."

"It seems like everywhere I turn despair is waiting to greet me."

"What, dear?"

"Trouble. It's become my second nature."

"Ah." Adele nodded as the wagon hit a deep pothole. "A body does have its share."

* * *

When Copper next opened her eyes she could see daylight peeking through the slit in the back canvas. Lingering smells of fried fatback and coffee permeated the air. From the sounds of things, folks were breaking camp and preparing for another day's travel.

Adele poked her head through the canvas opening. "Oh good. I was hoping you'd be awake. Can I bring you some tea and maybe a biscuit?"

Copper's stomach felt as empty as a big spender's pocket. She couldn't remember her last meal.

"A cup of tea would be nice."

Giving a nod, Adele dropped the canvas lining into place.

Hazy, Copper dozed while she awaited the drink. Her mind had yet to fully grasp her situation, and perhaps that was good. She might go mad if she fully comprehended her condition. Dr. Smith could wrap a simple injury, but it seemed Copper couldn't do anything simple. She thrived on complications. If the injury required special treatment from this Dr. Dyson, then she could indeed be in for a long recovery. Where would she find the funds to pay—yet hadn't Adele said Emily and Mackey's grandfather had ordered her care? She wasn't clear on that—and why would a stranger bother with her? She'd have to ask Adele to explain that when she was thinking straighter. This fuzziness was driving her insane!

She closed her eyes and the nightmares began.

The back canvas parted, and Josh Redlin stepped inside the wagon carrying a steaming cup.

Just the sight of that man sent her into spasms. She shook her head, warding off the nightmare. *Go away!*

"Mr. Redlin. Don't you think it's a little reckless on your part to stall out here so close to town? You could infect everyone here. Have you not considered the prospect?"

He turned cool eyes on her. "Sorry—I didn't catch your name."

"I didn't throw it."

The sick could use some nourishing broth, he'd said, looking her straight in the eye as though she wasn't working as hard and fast as she could to care for his ailing folk.

"Adele said you thought you might be able to drink a little something."

Oh dear Lord, spare me this horror. But the dream refused to lift. She could hear that man's voice as if he was standing in the wagon not fifteen feet away from her. He was either in her nightmares or he was actually there to torment her in person. From the hour he'd stopped that wagon train on the outskirts of Thunder Ridge with all those dead and dying people, he'd been a burr under her saddle.

Suddenly her thoughts were shockingly clear.

Heavens to Betsy. It wasn't a dream. He was here. In this wagon.

She hesitantly cocked one eye half open. There he stood, grinning like Asa Jeeters's old jackass after a meal of green grass.

"Miss Wilson. So we meet again."

With a groan, she clamped her eyes shut. Nightmare. That's all it was, and she would awaken any moment. *Wake up Copper! Open your eyes!*

She cautiously lifted an eyelid, then shut it.

This could not be happening.

Lord, I've endured it all—everything you've sent my way this past year. The war, the heavy rains, and Willow's injury. More rain. And mud. And burying parlors. But this is too much. I cannot go on. Take me now—no wait. Forgive me for my sins— those I know about and those I'm not aware that I committed. Okay. Now. Take me.

She waited. The scent of hot tea filled the wagon.

Okay. Now. Let's go.

"You're tea is getting cold."

Squeezing her eyes shut tighter, she pleaded. "Please . . . I beg you. Go away."

He sat down in the rocker, still holding the cup. "Now Miss Wilson. How can you be so thoughtless? Here I held up the wagon train until you could meet up with us, and you're still put out with me."

"Why would you hold up the wagon train?"

"When your foot was in more trouble than Dr. Smith could handle, Howard Matthews thought immediately of Dr. Dyson, who was in Fort Riceson. Since they knew the fort was on our way to Colorado, they thought to see whether we'd be willing to take you along. Of course, we'd already left Thunder Ridge. So we waited until you could catch up."

He continued. "If they'd had a better way—any other way, to get you there this time of the year, believe me when I say I would have found it for them. But they didn't, so drink your tea and listen up. I don't ordinarily speak to a woman in this tone, but even sick and flat on your back, you're not like most women. You're like a bad rash that won't let up, so here's the deal. There is no way in Hades that I'm going to take your abuse all the way to Fort Riceson. You will stay with Adele, and mind your manners and guard your tongue. I'll get you to the fort, see that you're made as comfortable as humanly possible, and I'll do this without one of us point-blank shooting the other—on the condition that you stay clear of me." He set the tea in her hands. "Now drink this, and go back to sleep."

"Why I . . . I . . . why . . ."

He pointed a finger. "I've been known to leave a body off at the nearest town if they give me trouble. Do you understand me, Miss Wilson? The delay has set the train back by at least a week and we're trying to outrun bad weather. We're doing you a favor. Accept it."

She opened her mouth to challenge him, then clamped it shut.

He nodded. "Just want you to know the rules. Now drink your tea." He got up, parted the canvas, and stepped out of the wagon.

Well, of all the unmitigated gall. He couldn't talk to her in that tone. She set the cup on the floor and threw back the quilt. She'd tell that man a thing or two. She swung her feet to the wagon floor and her head swam. Pain shot through her right ankle and the wagon spun in haphazard circles.

Falling back to the pallet, she fought hysteria. Josh Redlin? She would be subject to that . . . that brute until she was otherwise able to manage on her own?

That was sacrilege. She wouldn't stand for it. She would escape—find another wagon train going through Fort Riceson.

She would! She honestly would. The very moment she got enough strength to get up off this pallet.

Chapter 4

"Now what is this?" Adele's shrewd gaze focused on the cup of overturned tea. Dark liquid seeped from the cup onto the wagon floor.

Copper had aroused from her earlier oblivion. She'd dropped off to sleep the moment that maddening Redlin had given his "order" and left. Her insides churned with resentment. How could the good Lord put her smack into Josh Redlin's path? Hadn't the last few weeks been trying enough? The constant baiting, his testy remarks. She had reached the end of her rope with this man, and she sure didn't intend to spend another week in his company. She looked up to find Adele staring at her. "Well?"

"Well what?"

"How did you spill your tea? I'd wager you didn't drink a drop, did you?"

"I wouldn't drink anything Josh Redlin brought me. He probably poisoned it."

Tsking under her breath, Adele sank into the rocker and reached for her yarn. "I've never in my born days witnessed two grown folks spittin' venom at each other like you two."

"Talk to Mr. Redlin, not me. I've tried to tolerate the man and I can't."

"Can't or won't?" The rhythmic click of knitting needles filled the uncomfortable silence. "Seems to me you might owe the man a bit of gratitude. I'd say there wouldn't have been many that would have held up a wagon train for one little lady, especially since the weather's turned bad so early in the season."

"I didn't ask him to wait."

Adele shook her head. "You two better learn to get along. Forty miles is a far piece to argue."

"Jolie could set my foot. She could do it."

"That Arcadian woman that lives at the edge of Thunder Ridge? Some say she practices the devil's medicine."

"That's not true. She uses herbs and things." Copper was never sure of the "things," but sometimes the concoctions worked. At this point she was willing to try anything short of making this long arduous journey. Strength drained, she lay back, her right elbow resting on her forehead. "Take me back, Adele. I'll care for my ankle."

"And now how would I be doing that?"

"Arrange for a horse, and I'll ride back. We can't be too far from Thunder Ridge."

"No, I'd think it wouldn't be a far piece."

"I could make the ride."

She nodded. "I'd think you'd need to gain a little strength, but yes, you could make the ride."

Copper's spirit rose. "Then you'll do it?" *Saved.* Adele would spare her the agony of Redlin's company and almost certain clashes with the wagon master.

The woman's needles didn't miss a beat. "Oh no, I won't do it. I couldn't send you off to meet certain harm, but it's an interesting thought." She nodded agreeably. "It surely is."

Copper deflated. "But you said . . ."

"I didn't say anything, honey, you were doing all the talking and I was only agreeing. In theory you're not that wrong; there's only one hitch in your plan."

"And that is?"

"You'll be a cripple for life, or worse, you'll end up losing the foot."

The absurd implication took Copper's breath. Lose her foot? She tried to wiggle her right toes, and pain seared her efforts. "You're trying to scare me into submission, aren't you?"

Adele purled a stitch. "Honey, I didn't want to be the one to tell you, but Josh thinks that you need to know what you're up against, and he figures you won't listen to him." She lowered the needles and met Copper's gaze. "Lest you consider doing something foolish."

Foolish. How dare he think her a fool? Adele was clearly on Redlin's side. She needed a comrade, someone who'd stand up for her rights. "Where's Sadie?"

"Driving the wagon. We'll take turns switching off the reins. It's all been arranged. At night she'll sleep with the Sniders. They have more room in their rig."

Copper needed to talk to Sadie. She was a straight shooter. She wouldn't try to frighten her into compliance with Redlin's rules by telling tales of unthinkable speculations, even though the robust, good-natured woman had announced her intentions to snag the wagon master, and she most likely wouldn't want to anger Redlin. Still, Copper had to try.

"I want to see Sadie."

Adele nodded. "We'll be stopping for our noon meal shortly. I'll send her around."

"Make sure that you do." Copper's eyes drooped. "I want to talk to her. She'll help me."

"Oh, that she will; the woman's good as gold. If she takes a mind to help, you can be sure she'll do just that. Now why don't you rest? I'm going to make sure you eat a bite before this day is over if I have to spoon-feed you."

Over the noon break, Copper heard Sadie, a tall, raw-boned woman, part the back canvas. The lady was too commonplace to be considered pretty, but neither was she coyote ugly. She had a winsome smile, and was noted for her hard work.

"Yoo-hoo? Are you awake?"

Copper started, clearing her throat. "Come in, Sadie."

The woman stepped inside the wagon and approached the bedside. Copper didn't think she'd ever met a woman with such significant feet. She had to wear a man's large-sized boot. Dainty slippers would look like river barges on her.

"How ya doin', sweet thing?"

"Not so well." Self-pitying tears surfaced. With Sadie she'd have an ally—someone who would be on her side.

Sadie nodded. "To be sure—but we're praying real hard. Don't despair. Fort Riceson sits on the outskirts of Madison, Texas."

Copper forced back hysteria. Why did they talk as though she was dying! Other than the wretched pain in her ankle, she was perfectly fine when someone wasn't forcing laudanum down her throat.

"Sadie."

"Yes?"

"I need your help."

"Well certainly—anything, love. Do you need another blanket?" The woman turned to grab a wool throw. "Pillow? Something to eat? Back rub—a nice back rub would—"

"I need a horse."

Sadie paused. "We don't eat horse, dear. Now tonight we'll have a nice slab of beef and a few beans . . ."

"I want a horse to ride. And I need some rations, and warm clothing. Can you get me those things, and don't let anyone on the train know what you're doing?"

Sadie sank to the rocker. "Now why would you be needing such things? You're not going anywhere."

"I'm leaving. I'm going back to Thunder Ridge, and you have to help me. I'm not going to take any more pain medicine. When Adele brings it I'm going to hold it under my tongue and when she isn't looking I'm spitting it out. By tomorrow, my head should clear. I want you to have the horse and supplies ready. I'll make my break when we stop tomorrow night."

Nodding, Sadie listened intently.

"And above all, you are *not* to speak a word of this to Mr. Redlin. Do you understand?"

She nodded.

"Nor are you to tell anyone else my plans. Adele knows, but she won't try and stop me. And be sure that I have plenty of warm clothing and matches for a fire. It feels like it's getting very cold."

"Very," Sadie agreed.

Copper gritted her teeth and settled back on the pillow. It was time for more laudanum but she wouldn't take it. Adele had a sharp eye; she'd have to be very careful or the woman would catch on to her scheme. She'd pretend to sleep most of the day, which wouldn't be a stretch. She'd done nothing but sleep so she should be well rested for the arduous ride back to Thunder Ridge. There, Audrey and Willow would help her. Even if it meant calling Jolie to set the foot, it would be better than making the trek to Fort Riceson.

Adele stuck her head through the back opening. "We're about to pull out. Can I get you anything?"

Copper fought back nausea. The thought of food sickened her but she was weak as a newborn kitten. If her plan were to work she'd need nourishment. "I believe I could eat a bowl of broth, Adele."

The woman's face brightened. "I'll bring some right away."

"And tea—with lots of milk," Copper added, mentally retching.

"Well." Sadie shifted. "I'll be sitting with you this afternoon and we'll talk more, but you rest now. You hear?"

Absently nodding, Copper closed her eyes, drained. "Thank you, Sadie. I won't forget what you've done. You're a good person."

Sadie's voice drifted somewhere above her head. "Well thank you muchly, but I haven't done a thing, Miss Copper. Not a single thing."

The following night, Copper crept off her pallet. Her plan to not swallow the medicine worked like a charm—though wretched pain radiated from her ankle, creating no euphoria for what she was about to do.

Adele's snores filled the wagon as Copper eased to the back, carefully parting the canvas. Adele's sleepy voice came from the darkness. "Where you going, dearie?"

"Necessary—I have to use the necessary."

"The chamber pot is next to the wagon. I'll be glad to fetch it for you. You shouldn't be on that ankle."

"I'll be fine—go back to sleep."

Adele's answer came in the midst of a yawn. "Good night."

Scooting off the back gate, she gritted her teeth when fire shot through the injured ankle, white-hot lightning so intense it took her breath. Had she lost her mind? Just because she didn't like Redlin she was willing to risk all in order to escape him? The ludicrous thought lingered, but not for long. Yes, she was stubborn. Yes, she was risking a great deal, and if Willow or Audrey would try such a thing she'd have no trouble taking them to task about their foolish reasoning, but her friends weren't here, and her only aim, at this point, was to get to them, and they would help with her problem. She would not fall victim to Josh Redlin and his manner as long as she retained an ounce of breath. She could not, in her wildest dreams, understand why Willow and Audrey would send her off with Redlin in the first place.

You can do this, Copper. You must do this or face weeks on the trail with him and months after that away from your friends. Shuddering at the thought, she caught hold of the wagon and slipped around the corner. Families slept soundly under a bright harvest moon. Gritting her teeth, she released her hold and hobbled across the clearing, fighting pain so intense Adele's prior warning rang in her ears. *You could lose that foot.*

Still, Adele wasn't a doctor and Redlin could have concocted the dire situation to keep her under his thumb.

Horse. Where did Sadie wait with the horse, warm clothing, and food? Her eyes scanned unfamiliar shadows. She hadn't been out of the wagon since she'd been whisked through the night to join the train, and she should have been clearer on a meeting place.

She gave a low whistle and waited for a response. Seconds later she hooted softly, hoping she sounded somewhat like an owl. When a response failed to come, she gritted her teeth and moved toward a patch of mesquite. Halfway there she fell, smacking the rocky ground hard.

She sat up, determined to succeed. Though she hadn't swallowed a drop of the laudanum in twenty-four hours, the powerful painkiller lingered in her body and clouded her judgment. She sat up, and then shoved to her knees, tears coursing down her cheeks. The pain was so bad she couldn't think. How would she make the long ride to Thunder Ridge in the darkness? She couldn't. She'd have to endure long enough to find a town and send a wire for Caleb or Eli Gray to come with a wagon to get her.

Sadie wouldn't let her down, not Sadie. Willow had taken in Sadie and others when that horrible illness swept the train. She owed Willow and all the women of Thunder Ridge a debt of gratitude. Was that she, waiting right behind the bush?

Dropping to her knees, she crawled now, pulling herself along the frost-covered ground until her strength gave way and she collapsed on her face. She lay for a moment fighting defeat. She couldn't get there. She couldn't make it to the row of mesquite, and if she called out, her plan would be exposed.

Gathering grit, she dug her nails into the ground and pulled, easing her body an inch at a time. She could do this. But then the white-hot fire in her ankle rendered her light-headed. She couldn't faint; she would die of exposure in the falling temperatures and nobody knew she was out here. The sudden idiocy of her scheme came home to roost. She couldn't escape; she had barely enough strength to breathe. Burying her face in her hands, she awaited her fate. *Dear God, please let Willow and Audrey understand . . .*

"I'll bet you're looking for a horse."

Redlin. Why should she be surprised that he would be the one to find her? Not some kind, compassionate soul. Oh no. It had to be Josh. But the laugh was on him. She was dying. This hellish pain blistering her body could mean nothing less. So she would lie here and let him talk his fool head off and she'd say nothing. Mr. Smarty-pants knew everything, so surely Sadie had told him about the plan. Just let Sadie need something again and Copper wouldn't lift a hand to help—though she'd have no hand to lift. She'd be dead. The joke was on Redlin.

Josh's tone turned mystified. "Did I misinterpret? You did request a horse, warm clothing, and a couple of days' supplies?"

Copper rolled to her back and faced him. "And you, sir, were kind enough to bring them."

His gaze indicated the waiting animal beside him, the bulging saddlebags. "I think you'll find everything you need here."

She focused on him, squinting through one eye. "And now you're about to tell me that you're going to let me go."

He stood aside, affecting a gallant sweep. "Go with God."

It took a moment to decide if he was toying with her or if he was serious. Serious, she decided. She was free! He wasn't going to stop her! Clearing her throat, she asked. "Could you . . . help me aboard?"

"My pleasure." She suddenly found herself in his arms—arms that felt like steel bands—and sat in the saddle. He rechecked the cinch, and then lowered the stirrup. "Everything seems in order. Do you need a light?"

A lantern. She'd not thought that far. She'd have to have light. "Yes—thank you."

He indicated the item tied to the saddle. She stared at the heavy object. "What do I do with it?"

"Why, hold it." He smiled. "Moon's bright tonight, but who knows what tomorrow night will be." He stuck his hands in his front pockets and stared up at a brilliant sky. "Ring around the moon. Rain's coming in. I packed a slicker for you."

Now how was she going to hold a heavy lantern, control the horse, and hang on the saddle pommel when she barely had the strength to exhale? With a sinking heart, she knew that she couldn't. She couldn't ride through unfamiliar terrain in the darkness, holding a lantern.

Again he had bested her.

"Well now, you have a good ride home, Miss Wilson." He turned his collar up. "That storm will likely turn to snow but it'll melt the minute it hits the ground, but then in these parts you just never know. Could be knee-deep by morning and it could miss us and head north, but I'd be sure and build a fire every night to keep the wolves at bay—those pesky critters can get mighty ugly when they're hungry." He removed his hat. "Ma'am, I wouldn't feel right sending you off like this unless I remind you of the snakes—'course it's getting a little cold for the rattlers but you can never be too careful. If they get your horse then you're on foot, and that would be troublesome. Trying to pack a bedroll and food—that's tough, but if you're lucky you'll run into men on the road—but here again I'm presuming to tell you what to do and I do know how you don't take kindly to that sort of thing. Now, some of those men are the mean sort. Real mean." He settled his hat back on his head. "Guess that's about it. You be sure and wrap up tightly because if snow moves in, a body can freeze to death in the elements."

By now Copper had lain over the saddle pommel and was staring blankly up at him. The cad. He was going to let her ride off to face certain death—a woman alone. A woman in so much pain she wanted to roll on the ground and tear her hair out by the roots.

"Well." He lifted his hand to smack the horse's flank, sending her on her way. "Have a safe trip."

"Stop!" She barely recognized her voice, but she knew she'd yelled. She broke into sobs. She hurt so badly.

Redlin gently gathered her into his arms, and she buried her face in his warm shoulder and let her emotions come.

His voice was warm against her temple. "I know you detest me, Copper, but I am not the enemy. I'm trying to help you." He paused, lifting her chin, forcing her to look at him. Hot tears coursed down her cheeks. "You're a sensible woman. What I'm going to tell you isn't meant to frighten you, but you have to know the severity of your wound. The injury is so grave that you could lose your foot unless it's handled properly. Infection might set in, but isn't likely at this point since there's no break in the skin, but Dr. Smith doesn't know what we're dealing with. Dr. Dyson will."

Her face nestled deeper into his buckskin jacket as the frightening words penetrated. She would be a cripple. She didn't want to live.

"There's an excellent doctor in Fort Riceson, and Matthews believes this man can save the limb."

"My ankle isn't infected now?"

His tone gentled. "It doesn't appear to be. That's why we can't waste time going on wild-goose chases. Let's get to the fort first and see what Dyson says." His gaze met hers in the moonlight. "Can we please call a truce in this insane feud between us? Will you stop fighting me and help me get you to Fort Riceson and back to good health?"

She was so exhausted his plea barely touched the corner of her mind, but she understood the animosity must stop. If she was to have any chance to save the foot, she had to swallow her pride and get along.

"Nod if you agree."

She nodded.

"Then let's get you back to Adele's wagon. She has a hot water bottle waiting for you."

"Can I have two spoons of laudanum tonight?"

"Adele tells me you haven't been swallowing the ones she's given you. There's a precious, limited supply."

"I won't spit it out again." That she could promise if this dreadful pain would only cease.

"I'll speak to Adele. We'll keep you comfortable."

Josh Redlin might be the most maddening man the good Lord ever put on this earth, but at that moment Copper thought he was very close to being an angel.

And she would swallow every beloved drop of laudanum. That was one promise she would have no trouble keeping.

Chapter 5

The wagon creaked over the rutted terrain. Copper lay on her pallet thinking that she had seen enough canvas ceiling to last a lifetime. Lying flat on her back all day staring up at a wagon roof was enough to send a body mad. The compresses Adele applied to the injured ankle three times a day helped, but the throbbing never let up. Pain was a constant companion, and the laudanum was now limited to nighttime use. Because of her folly, she'd wasted some of the precious supply, and now she had to tolerate the anguish until evenings when she could take the medication and drop into oblivion.

She'd spent most of this morning dressing. What used to be a ten-minute duty had turned into a two-hour ordeal. First she would pull on her pantaloons and then her dress. Then sit for ten minutes to gain enough strength to button the bodice. Lacing up her shoe and then brushing her hair left her exhausted. She had to lie down to recuperate.

By the noon hour, she was ready and intent on rejoining the world. She had determined on that frightful night Redlin had carried her, helpless and terrified, back to Adele's wagon that she would not give that man another moment's trouble. If it killed her, she would keep her thoughts and criticisms to herself and simply pray for him—for surely if any man needed her prayers, it was he. She'd not seen him in a couple of days and she was grateful she didn't have to face his glee that her plan had fallen flatter than a pancake.

Most had eaten their fare of cold soda biscuits and fat pork when she eased from the back of the wagon. Some chose to spread the biscuit with thick beans that had jelled overnight. Either fare stemmed hunger and kept the travelers eager for a hot supper. Eyes turned to acknowledge her appearance. A couple of men sprang to their feet and came to her assistance but she brushed the help aside.

"Thank you, but I have to learn to manage, and I'd prefer to do this on my own." When the words came out more stridently than she intended, she softened the objection. "You are very kind, but please, I need to do this alone."

The men nodded and stepped back as she slowly hobbled to where women and children grouped. Adele and Sadie stood up, but Copper waved their help aside. "I thought I'd enjoy a few minutes of fresh air." Her eyes focused on Redlin, who was engrossed with Frank Richardson, second in command. Josh glanced her way, frowned, but continued with his conversation.

Copper dropped down on a fallen tree trunk and set aside the crutches Sadie had dropped by the wagon last night, saying they'd belonged to her deceased husband, and she had no use for them. At the time Copper had seriously doubted that she would ever have use for them, but a new day often brought new hope, and this day she'd wakened with fresh determination. Now Eli wouldn't have to make her a pair.

When she looked up she encountered so many pairs of eyes focused on her she burst out laughing. "You look like you've seen a ghost."

Uneasy snickers broke out. Adele said, "We're just not used to seeing you up and about. Shouldn't you be . . . ?"

"Sleeping? No. If I'm ever to survive this ordeal, I'll have to help with the process." She smiled. "Please, don't let me disturb you." She drew her shawl closer against a bitter cold wind. "I'll visit a moment and then return to the wagon."

"We'll be pulling out shortly," an older woman observed. "Take care that you don't catch a chill."

Copper's gaze traveled to a small cluster of children huddled around a tree base. Wind ruffled the pages of the open book a teenage girl was reading. Rapt eyes focused on her. She inclined her head toward the gathering. "What's going on?"

"That's Reba. She's reading to the children like she does every day at the noon hour."

They seemed to be enjoying it immensely. From this distance Copper recognized the title: *Tom Brown's Schooldays*.

"Oh, the young'uns love it." This came from Lil, trying to control her young toddler. "Reba tries to school the children, but she's not trained, not like Laura Fedderson. Laura was an educated teacher."

"Why isn't Miss Fedderson teaching the children now?"

"The Feddersons had to drop out of the train shortly after

we pulled out. She had this awful cough, and it worsened. Her husband thought it best to take her back home until she fully recovered." The woman shook her head. "Near broke Laura's heart. She was looking forward to a new start, moving to a better climate. They lived with her husband's folks, and Laura longed for a home of her own."

Copper's gaze was drawn to the children's studious faces, and she was reminded of her class. Little Mackey. Emily and Harold. What were they doing now? Would Beeder's Cove resume school without her? Of course they would. They'd find a replacement until she was back. Being a cripple didn't mean that she was a freak or couldn't work. Once, when she was a child, she saw a man whose feet were so twisted that he had to be pushed in a chair with wheels on it. Copper remembered how she'd recoiled at the sight. Would people look at her with the same pity? She would have both feet, but how severe would her limp be? Would folks stare at her in pity? One of the ladies pitched the last of the coffee on the fire. "Miss Wilson? You're a teacher, aren't you?"

Adele answered before Copper could. "The finest! Why, that's how she injured her ankle. Bravest thing I'd ever heard. Fire broke out in the schoolroom, and Copper got all the children out alive and well. Why, she even defied the inferno and went back into the building and pulled two of the youngest to safety."

Murmurs of approval circulated.

"It was nothing," Copper said. "Any teacher would have done the same."

"Still," Sadie praised, "it was a heroic thing you did. And now with that injury—"

Copper broke in before Sadie could make a prediction that she didn't want to hear. "My, the wind is brisk today."

"Josh says it's gonna be a bad winter this year. The geese are flying ahead of time, and the tree bark is awfully thick. We could be in for an ugly one."

The women started breaking camp. "Praise the good Lord we should be in Colorado in another few weeks. Maybe the heaviest snows will stay well to the north of us."

Copper insisted on making the short trek back to Adele's wagon alone, though her ankle screamed with misery. After two tries, she managed to negotiate the step into the wagon and drop to the pallet, staring at the canvas top, which strangely didn't look as tedious at it had half an hour earlier.

While the travelers checked rigging and axles, Copper considered the children on the wagon train. How many were gathered beneath the tree? Ten? Twelve? She thought the young lady reading the book was quite articulate, and the interest shining in the children's eyes inspiring. She missed seeing young, fresh faces eager for knowledge, at least most of them. But in time, even the reluctant ones could be introduced to a subject that would grab their attention, and the world would open to them.

The call of "Wagons roll" sounded from the head of the train, and rig by rig the command went down the line. Sadie gave a whistle and the wagon lurched. Copper clamped her jaw in pain, but willed her thoughts back to the children. She could teach. She could lie here day after day or she could work past the ache and offer to give a simple lesson at noon hour. She didn't have books, or rulers, or chalk, or a board, but she had a sound mind the Lord had given her, and a good education Papa had provided.

So what will it be, Copper? Lie here and wallow in self-pity? Or do something worthwhile.

The answer came surprisingly easily.

Only one problem troubled her. She hadn't factored Josh Redlin into the equation.

The wagon train rumbled over rain-soaked trails, and she mulled over the best way to approach the ogre without upsetting him. She had no doubt that he was true to his word, and if she caused him an ounce of trouble he'd set her off at the next town, though strangely enough he had indulged her earlier break for freedom. Maybe Sadie had influenced his thinking. The woman clearly wanted that man, even though Redlin was younger than she. Sadie didn't seem to fit with the wagon master, yet stranger things had happened.

After supper, Copper once again eased from the wagon and set off to find the testy wagon master. The crutches were clumsy and made her armpits sore. She stumbled more than she walked. This was so humiliating. She must have made a pretty sight when she found him beside the chuck wagon, shaving. Flushed, hair hanging loose, she leaned on a support and waited for him to notice her. Finally his eyes briefly acknowledged her and he continued his task, focused on the mirror hanging from a tree limb.

"This makes twice that you've been on that ankle today. Do you think that's wise?"

"I'm not putting my weight on it. I use the other foot."

"Whatever."

"May I approach you?" She felt like a lowly servant begging permission to approach the king.

He remained focused on his chore. "I thought we had an agreement."

"We do, but since you're boss . . ." Oh, how she hated to admit his superiority. "I'll be forced to consult you from time to time."

He bent to run the straight razor closer to his nose, and she could have sworn he was grinning. "What's on your mind?"

She explained about the noon meal and witnessing the children's rapt interest in knowledge, or at least in the book *Tom Brown's Schooldays.*

When she finished her presentation she held her breath. He'd refuse her. He was just ornery enough to make the children suffer because he didn't like her.

He straightened, absently wiping cream off his face. "Do you feel up to giving a lesson every day?"

"I'm in pain, but I refuse to lie in that wagon and be medicated all the way to Fort Riceson. I would very much appreciate the opportunity to do something to pass the time."

He set the razor aside, and reached for a towel. "That's right admirable of you, Miss Wilson."

"Then you'll permit me to teach?"

"If you feel up to the task, I have no objection. The mothers on the train should be very grateful."

"I haven't spoken to anyone but you about this."

He winked. "You're learning."

There it was; the tone. That maddening pitch like he was her father and she was a willful child. "Learning what?"

"You're learning you can catch more flies with honey than vinegar."

Vinegar indeed.

"You do like to gloat, don't you?"

"Miss Wilson."

She clamped down on her tongue. Turning her back on him, she shuffled off, but not before she stuck her tongue out at him.

If it hadn't been for that dratted shaving mirror nailed on the tree, she'd have gotten away with it too.

Chapter 6

So once again Copper turned a page in her Book of Life. She had found renewed purpose, and if there was one essential ingredient to life, it was purpose, a solid reason to get up every dawn and start afresh.

She spent the afternoon jotting down items she needed for her small school. Among the wagon train some families would have books, and others would have pencils and paper. The proposed school would have juniper and peachleaf willows for walls, the sky for a roof, and God's good earth for flooring. There'd be no warm building in which to educate the children, but it would have a woman's desire to shape youthful insights to a higher standard. She could hardly wait to tell Audrey and Willow of the new event. Setting the tablet aside, she reached for the plain white linen paper Adele had encouraged her to use and began a letter to her two best friends.

Dearest Willow and Audrey,

Though it's been a short while, it feels like years since I've seen you. Willow, the wedding was beautiful. I know you wanted a large extravaganza, but heartfelt vows given in earnest are the ultimate expression of love. I wish both you and Tucker endless years of the God-given love that you experienced at the exact moment you pledged your all to each other. The older I get, the more I realize love is not a given; that not everyone will find their soul mate. But if they do they are given a blessing almost beyond human comprehension. So my dear loved one, may God go with you and your new husband.

Audrey, I've been told that you sat with me shortly after the fire. I'm sorry, I have no recollection of your presence but I thank you dearly. You have been so in my heart of late. I know you worry about my ankle, but please don't. Just pray for me and my recovery. Now that your eyes have been opened to love, my prayers are answered regarding Eli and his feelings for you. I feared that perhaps God might have to send a burning bush to awaken him, but apparently he'd noticed you all along. Actually, I'm a bit envious of you. Even I could love that gentle man, but I believe he was meant for you, dear one. You, and you alone. But sometimes it takes more than good eyesight to make proper choices. What's the Scripture? Ecclesiastes—there is a time and a place for everything.

I know you're both awaiting my news, and I have very little to tell. The ankle is gravely injured (as I'm sure you were told), and there is a possibility that if infection were to set in I could lose the foot. The thought is indeed tragic, but I suppose that's why the good Lord gave me a spare. One foot is better than none, and I console my anxiety by remembering the brave young men who came through the war and lost both feet. But now to the best news. Redlin has given me permission to hold a small class during noon meals. Of course we only stop long enough to eat and refresh our needs, but I plan to prepare five-minute lessons that will stick with the children. I am very excited about the prospects since it will fill many long hours and I hope enlighten the children.

I have medication at night, but it clouds my thinking and causes night sweats and nightmares.

Speaking of which, I will now address my guess to what's uppermost in your minds: "Has she shot Josh Redlin yet?" or "Has Josh shot her?" Neither of the above, I'm happy to report. We've made a pact; I stay out of his way and he will get me safely to the doctor at the fort.

There have been a few minor skirmishes, but so far we've remained adult about our situation. Adele tells me I owe Josh a debt of gratitude for holding the wagon train. Of course Howard Matthews factors greatly in the whole process, for without his financial generosity I would be lying abed without the slimmest hope of full recovery.

I must close now. It's nearing four o'clock, the hour the wagon train stops every night. We camp close to water, so tonight I will ask Adele if I might take a full bath.

I'll write as often as prudent, but I haven't asked when or how the mail goes out. I suppose if it doesn't you won't be reading this anyway.

She drew a funny face at the bottom of the page, then laid the pencil aside, folded the missive, stuck it into an envelope, and addressed it.

At the moment, she'd give all she had (which admittedly included the sum of four dresses, pantaloons, and two pairs of wool stockings) to spend five minutes with her two best friends. Just a few precious minutes to feel their arms around her, encouraging her, lending her hope that had began to fade even as she prayed for strength and acceptance.

Friends might fail. They might stumble and cause hurt, but when it came right down to it, a friend, a true friend, was better than a peppermint stick on Christmas morning, and right now Copper craved some emotional sweetness.

A hot bath might be as comforting as a best friend, Copper decided that evening as she sank into a tub of steaming water. Adele had a couple of men haul a wooden tub into the wagon, and then she and Sadie filled it full of hot and cold water. The weather had turned mild, almost warm. "Indian summer," she'd heard one of the alternate drivers say at noon. There were two such young men on the train. They had drifted into Thunder Ridge a week or so before she left. They seemed harmless enough, but still the people of the town were suspicious of them. Seemed they had approached Redlin just moments before the train pulled out and told him they wanted to see Colorado. He had told them if they were willing to do their share of the work for the grub alone, they could come along. They had nothing to lose so they grabbed the chance, earning their keep by standing guard at night and helping drive wagons when needed.

"Don't get that right foot wet," Sadie cautioned as she was about to leave. "And don't sit there so long you'll take a chill."

Copper dutifully promised, but her body had now descended to heaven. A warm, soapy heaven.

An hour later, she eased from the wagon, feeling (and smelling) as fresh as a blooming lilac bush in spring. Even her step was livelier. She knew the mild night air would dry the thick damp hair that hung loose to her waist. She had the letter to Willow and Audrey tucked under her left arm, hoping to find Redlin close to the fire. Of course he wasn't. He was off three hundred feet down the small stream with the other men doing their nightly shooting, an exercise that made sure the weapons were freshly loaded and the caps would be sure to fire. The ritual was nerve-wracking and the loud reports never failed to startle her, but she knew the practices were necessary; all guns were kept loaded and ready. After supper, the men would usually hang around and do some additional target practice. Out of sheer boredom, she often watched the ritual. The males would go off downstream and pick a snag or some target and fire away. The revolvers and rifles were all muzzle-loading, cap-and-ball affairs. Redlin, of course, had to be different. He carried one of the new Henry rifles that could hold sixteen rounds. There were only three such rifles on the wagon train; most of the men were forced to pour powder down the muzzle and then ram a ball home. To fire the gun, a cap was put on the tube to ignite the charge. With a Henry, you had to pull out a long rod, put in the cartridges, and then replace the rod. After that, however, sixteen shots could be fired in rapid succession and the weapon could be loaded hours or days prior to use. Even to Copper, who knew little about firearms, the advantages of the repeating Henry were obvious.

As she approached, the sounds of men's laughter and bragging skipped across the water.

"Hey Franklin! I'll bet you a fried chicken supper I can reload faster than you can."

"I don't know where you're going to get any fried chicken around here, but you're on, Harrison!"

Copper winced as two guns blasted away simultaneously. Then, just a few seconds later, the two roared again, one just a little before the other. "I guess I just saved some poor old hen's life," came the triumphant shout.

Josh spotted her and broke away from the good-natured ribbing. He walked up the embankment, Henry in hand.

"They say," she began, "that muzzle loaders are more accurate at a short distance."

He paused, removing his hat, absently dusting the brim on his thigh. "I'm not sure what 'they' you're referring to, but folks 'say' anything."

"You prefer the Henry?"

"I do."

"If a buffalo was heading straight for you intent on trampling you to death, would you have time to shoot twice?"

"I'd sure be quick as I could."

She shrugged. Why would she care if a buffalo trampled him?

"What aren't you in camp with the other women?"

"I have a question."

His eyes lightly but politely skimmed her. "I don't know what you've done, but you smell good."

Heat tinged her cheeks with the uncommon observation.

She would have thought she could run through camp with her hair on fire and he wouldn't notice—or care. "Thank you. I took a bath."

She met his laughing eyes and felt the blush deepen. He was certainly exhibiting more manly tendencies than ogre characteristics tonight.

"Like lilacs in spring."

"Yes, Sadie had some scented soap." She cleared her throat, aware that he didn't look so bad himself. The warm weather had brought out the men's grooming tendencies. Earlier she had heard them splashing and cavorting in the river. "Anyway, I was wondering about mail."

"What about it?"

"I wish to send a letter to Willow and Audrey." She leaned on her crutch and drew the envelope from under her left arm. "Where can I mail it?"

"At the first local stage station you see."

She frowned. She hadn't seen anything but bushes, rocks, and mesquite. "And where might that be?"

"Mike has the responsibility of mailing letters for the entire train at the first opportunity."

Mike. One of the younger men who'd joined up in Thunder Ridge. "Thank you. Do I need to leave the letter with you?"

"Nope. He'll give a mail call the night before."

"Thank you."

"You're welcome."

She turned and hobbled toward camp when she heard him say under his breath. "Yes sir, you sure do smell mighty good."

Chapter 7

⌒

The following noon, Copper gathered the children. Since time was short, she permitted them to eat while she taught. She'd hope to find subjects that interested both girls and boys, and the first lesson was one they'd be sure to repeat during the long afternoon ride.

She introduced herself, told a little about her previous teaching background, and explained her intent to give short but meaningful lessons that she hoped would remain with them. Her goal had never altered from the time she'd taught her first class. She wanted the child to absorb not just information, but come away with a real thirst for knowledge.

She'd heard chatter among the children about the Indians. With the cessation of hostilities between North and South, this aspect of life on the plains was particularly worrisome. Any number of men had left the service of both militaries with their need for violence unabated. Some had fallen in with the Indians, stirring them up and fanning resentments. The children's most graphic worry was of scalping, not a pleasant thought for anyone, but especially frightening to the young ones. And one that every man was determined to protect against.

When every eye focused on her, she said, "Today I want to talk about fear. Rational fear versus irrational fear."

"What's the difference?" a bigger boy asked. "If you're afeared you're afeared."

"There is a difference," she said. "And we're going to discuss some examples."

Cold biscuits forgotten, the children waited for her to explain. Copper knew scalping was openly discussed among families, but she wondered if parents spent more time on dire warning than simple reasoning. They had passed several crude crosses that marked Christian burials. It took little imagination to blame the natives, even though it was more likely that the deaths were due to disease or accident. So it was easy for the children to believe that all Indians were death threats. After all, weren't all snakes poisonous?

"Not all Indians are bad," she began. And she had their undivided attention.

She continued, "Once when I was a little girl, I wandered away from our homestead. Of course I'd been warned to stay close to the house, but it was a beautiful day and I could hear the gurgling creek inviting me to take off my shoes and stockings and enjoy the cool water. I had a most lovely time, but then I looked up to see seven warriors, all decked out in feathers and paint. Well, my mother's and father's warning came back straightaway and I was terrified. I knew if I didn't run as fast as I could my scalp would be hanging from one of those brave's belts. So I ran as fast and as hard as I could, screaming at the top of my lungs. My folks near died of fright when I lunged through the open doorway shouting, 'Indians!' My father just reached for his gun and met the braves on the front porch. To my surprise, they were laughing. Just sitting on their ponies holding their sides in laughter. Of course they knew I was convinced that they'd come to scalp me." She sighed. "I got the scare of my life that morning, but all they wanted was sugar and coffee. A pound of sugar can go a long way in trading with the Indians."

Smiling, she looked around the group. "The knowledge that I want to leave you with today is this: Fear is good, but knowledge is better. The white man is beginning to move into the land the Indians have owned and lived on for hundreds of years. They are afraid we will kill all the buffalo that they need. Some of them are being sent to reservations where they must remain for the rest of the lives. So they fear us, just as we fear them. Some of them are indeed our enemies, but some of them are probably friendly."

One round-eyed child blinked. "How can we tell the difference?"

Copper bit her lower lip. How did one tell the difference? She realized that in an attempt to allay needless fears she might have planted a seed of trust that would someday ill serve one of the children. She was thankful to hear the call, "Roll 'em out!"

Tomorrow she'd stick with geography.

After supper two days later, Mike made the mail call.

Several had letters to give him. Sadie took Copper's letter to save her some painful steps. For some reason the swelling in the ankle had been worse for a couple of days, and she suspected she might be overdoing. The nightly hot packs and laudanum barely kept the pain in check. Yesterday she'd braved a peek when Adele changed the bandage and felt faint. The terrible swelling seemed more troubling than the pain, but Adele's practiced eye predicted infection hadn't set in. Redlin hadn't asked, but Copper figured Sadie or Adele kept him well advised of her condition.

Mike stopped to sit beside her for a while as the others gathered their correspondence. He was a friendly sort, hailing from Ireland. His cheery accent lifted Copper's sprits. She loved to hear him say, "Top o' the mornin' to ya!" as his way of saying "Good day!" or "Hello!" She noticed he used the greeting in the afternoon as well.

"And a fine evening it is, Miss Wilson."

"That it is, Mike. A most enjoyable respite." The waxing moon had been shedding increasingly bright light for several nights and tonight it fairly bathed the campsite; the stars on the other side of the sky were as bright as glistening icicles suspended overhead.

He turned pensive. "Hard to conceive, it is, that this same moon shines on my folks."

Copper lifted her eyes to study the magnificent sight. Right now Audrey and Willow went about their regular routine beneath that same moon. Yet the distance between her and her friends seemed even more remote than the distance between her and the twinkling stars. "I understand you're from Dublin?"

"That I am, but I try to speak only good English—and I'm doing a wee bit of fine job, wouldn't you say?"

"Oh . . . to be certain." She grinned.

Mail began to arrive and Mike put the letters in a leather satchel. One by one a family member would hand him an envelope, and their expressions told that homesickness occupied minds tonight. Many had left mothers, fathers, brothers, and sisters, some whom they might never see again. Even Redlin dropped a letter beside the young Irish lad. It was all Copper could do to contain her sudden interest. *Now whom would he be writing a letter to?*

Frank Richardson whistled, and Mike sprang to his feet and trotted to the Richardson wagon.

Easing closer to the leather bag, Copper bent, trying to read the upside-down address on Redlin's correspondence. Drats. His penmanship was disgraceful.

She smiled hello to a couple of latecomers and nudged the satchel wider open with the toe of her boot to accept their post. When the couple moved on she bent and quickly flipped the wagon master's letter right-side up, the address now easily readable.

Mrs. Susan Farris
31 Front Street
Dallas, Texas

Susan Farris. Love interest? Couldn't be his wife, or he would address her as Susan Redlin. Sister? Niece? Could be his mother, but the last names weren't the same.

Mike trotted back and dropped a handful of envelopes into the sack. By now it was getting late and folks were heading to their wagons.

The great mystery would have to wait until another time. Copper reached for her crutches and eased to her feet. She dreaded the effects of the laudanum, yet craved the relief it brought. She hadn't thought to ask about the remaining distance to Fort Riceson. She dearly hoped it wasn't too great because Dr. Smith said time was of the essence. She recalled that phrase recurring over and over in her confused state.

How long could a person live in this pain and not go mad?

She wasn't sure, and she surely did not want to find out.

Chapter 8

Mid-morning, a Risher and Hall Stage Line galloped by the wagon train. Four cavalrymen rode in front and four more rode in back. The stage line's brilliant red, green, and yellow colors were striking. The coach had striped spokes and doors, with a canvas-covered trunk and baggage rack.

Copper had decided to ride up front and avoid much of the boredom of travel. This afternoon Sadie was at the reins. Blissful snores floated from the back. Adele was asleep in her rocker, taking advantage of the break.

Sadie shook her head. "Wonder where those folks are going in such a hurry."

"Doesn't seem that an animal could keep up that pace for very long." Copper's eyes fixed on the six fine matched horses with silver mounting fixtures with white rings and a brilliantly colored tassel hanging from the cheek piece of the bridle. The driver wore gauntlet gloves with a long braided lash whip in his right hand, and when he swung it over his head it sounded like a pistol shot.

"An animal can't," Sadie said. "I read all I could get my hands on afore we left home, and one paper said stage stations are somewhere between twelve and fifteen miles apart so the drivers change teams. Risher and Hall has one of the largest mail and stage lines in Texas."

"Why the cavalry escort?"

Sadie shook her head. "They're protection. If the stage runs into Indians and the like, the escorts fall back and fight while the stage driver does his best to get to the nearest military post."

"That's frightening. Couldn't that be miles and miles away?"

Sadie shrugged. "There's a post built every hundred miles or so, but I'd think you could be in a heap of trouble if you were on one of those stages and ran into a band of Comanches or Kiowas."

"Now Sadie, didn't you hear my lesson about fear?"

"Shore did, and sorry but I can't agree. I don't fancy seeing my scalp dangling from one of those redskins' belts. If one approaches this gal, she's heading in the opposite direction just as fast as she can run."

Copper chuckled, recalling her childhood encounter and the fright of seeing those braves staring down at her from horses that looked to be tall as pine trees.

"Them savages don't fight like us," Sadie said. "They swoop in on their ponies and the arrows fly, then they turn tail and gallop off for all they're worth and outrun the gunshots. They won't stand and fight, though I'd have to say I can't much blame them."

"Some of them have guns, don't they, like we do?"

Sadie made a *poosh* sound with her mouth. "Stolen, usually. From what I hear they ain't much danger with a gun. They carry G.D. caps—cheap ammunition. The caps will shoot all right in dry weather, but they aren't worth a lick in wet weather. There's been many a red man picked off before he could reload."

Copper took note of the dark cloud bank that hung low in the northern sky when the wagon train pulled into evening camp. The past couple of days Indian summer held with mild and even warm temperatures.

Today Sadie's was the first wagon in line. Redlin put his horse into a stiff gallop and rode in a large circle. Sadie fell in behind, and the camping ritual began. As soon as the other rigs formed a circle the teams were brought to a stop. Wagons were drawn up with the front wheels beside the hind wheels of the rig in front. The ritual served two purposes; to know how to group if attacked, and to form a stock corral. A space about a wagon length formed a gate. As soon as stock was unhitched, the herders took them out to graze until sundown, then they were driven back inside the wagon corral for the night. Precautionary ropes were tied from wagon to wagon so that the stock couldn't escape or be stolen by the Indians. Redlin's train had about twenty extra horses and fifteen additional mules.

Men dug the nightly trench and a fire was started. Sometimes wood was available; if not, buffalo chips were used. By sundown the air had filled with scents of beans seasoned with a big hunk of fat pork, bread cooking in a Dutch oven, and pots of sauce made from dried fruit.

Tonight the wagons were camped within seeing distance

of a stage station. After supper Mike announced that he was taking the mail. He glanced at Copper, who had just made it back from the small stream where she'd taken a sponge bath. "Would you like to come along, Miss Wilson?"

She would love to come along, but she knew that even the short walk was beyond her capacity.

"I'll put you sidesaddle on a horse and lead the animal," he offered.

"You would?" Her heart quickened. The outing would be delightful. The mild night air made it a perfect evening to do something at least a little entertaining. It would be a much welcome respite from the dreary routine.

Redlin glanced up with a frown when Copper passed him, assisted by Mike. She thought it might be nice to explain, to allay his curiosity, but then realized that she didn't want to be nice. Not to him.

Mike lifted her onto the horse and took her crutches, carrying them with the mail sack.

Moonlight drenched the path as the young lad led the animal to the outpost. As they drew near, she noted the activity. A group of soldiers, evidently the ones who accompanied the stages, loitered in front of the outpost. When Mike led the animal to the railing, the entire group of men stood to their feet and removed their hats.

Copper smiled. The men were young, most fine-looking. She wished Audrey were here, but then knew it wouldn't matter. Her friend had eyes only for Eli Gray now. Copper was the lone spinster of the group, but she was so pleased with the happiness her friends had found.

Mike lifted her off the horse, handed her the crutches, and they entered the station, Copper trying to appear that she was at complete ease with the wooden supports. As Mike delivered the mailbag, a private coach arrived. Moving to the window, Copper watched the activity until Mike led her over to the station attendant, pointing out the strange heart-shaped candy box on the counter.

"Mighty pretty, isn't it?" The clerk held up the flowery box. "Designed by Richard Cadbury, for Valentine's Day." A nearby soldier took it from the clerk and patted his treasure. "I won the chocolates from a gentleman in a hand of poker. Taking it back to my wife when I get leave next month."

"It's most exquisite," Copper noted. And she'd bet the creams and bonbons inside were pure heaven.

Finally Mike said they'd best be getting back to camp. When they exited the small building, ten grinning soldiers awaited Copper, two of them holding the mare's reins.

She glanced at Mike and smiled. "Why thank you, gentlemen." Mike stepped up and lifted her into the saddle, then took the crutches. There was an unspoken, but not to be ignored, curiosity concerning the supports and injury. She explained about the accident, and that she was on her way to Fort Riceson to have it looked after. Finally, Mike led the horse away, leaving the young men with hats off and eyes focused on her.

When they approached the outside corral, the guard called out, "Who goes there?"

"Friend of the guard!" Mike returned. Any other answer would risk a nervous sentry shooting first and asking questions later.

Inside the camp perimeter, Mike lifted Copper off the mare and led the animal to the corral.

A male voice sounded from the shadows. "Out a little late, aren't you, Miss Wilson?"

She turned to see Redlin leaning against the back of Adele's wagon, looking better than any man had a right to look after a long day's ride.

She glanced up, assessing the sky. "No, I don't believe that I am, Mr. Redlin." She smiled. "Is there a curfew?"

He slowly removed a piece of straw he'd been chewing on, his eyes skimming her lazily. "No curfew. Just thought it was time most folks were in bed. Cavorting with soldiers leaves a bad taste in some of the women's mouths."

"Cavorting!" Steam built in her brain. She lowered her voice. Sadie and Adele were most likely asleep for the night, but she couldn't be sure. "What woman even *hinted* at indiscretion?" she whispered harshly. "Tell me this instant, I'll go set her straight right now. I accompanied Mike to mail the—" She stopped. "Wait a minute. How do you know where I've been?" Was he spying on her? What right did he have to guard her like she was a prisoner?

He kept his tone low but to the point. "It's my business to know where my people are, and like it or not, you're one of my people at the moment."

"At the moment. Speaking of which, how much longer do I have to endure you?"

"Well, let me see. If it doesn't become a downpour in the next couple of days, which it looks like it might, we'll be at the fort in three days or so."

She crossed her arms, allowing one crutch to fall. *Here we go again. Why hadn't she held her tongue? Now he'd bait her, and she would be ripe for the catch.*

"Of course, heavy rain will make the river crossing between here and the fort a bit more difficult. The Buffalo can get pretty ugly this time of year if it's up and running. We have twenty-five rigs to get across. Should that happen it will be more like five or six days before we reach the fort. But—and I only mention this niggling little worry because I feel obligated to warn you about the possibility of further delay—there's the prospect of more holdup if a horse goes lame, or a wheel breaks. Then we're looking at—"

"All right! I understand." Just like Redlin. Delay. Delay. She drew a tolerant breath. "If a horse goes lame or a wagon wheel breaks, couldn't we just keep going and leave someone behind to help?"

But of course not. Not Josh Redlin, who had the audacity to stop this very wagon train—with ill and dying people—not two hundred feet outside Thunder Ridge. He'd keep the entire train together and moving forward at all costs.

He shifted, lifting his hat to smooth his hair. "No ma'am. These Indians are a temperamental sort; no one can predict their behavior. Sort of reminds me of you, in some ways. They like nothing better than to scatter a train or raid a straggler."

She propped her crutch beside the wagon and decided to ignore the taunt. The night's outing had put her in a good mood. The reaction of the men at the stage stop proved they still found her attractive. She wouldn't bother to rise to this jackanapes's bait. Soon she'd be rid of the nuisance named Redlin.

Turning, she tried to pull herself into the wagon bed. She heaved.

Then grunted. Pain shot up her right leg.

A masculine arm slipped around her waist and hoisted her

aboard. "You're going to have to be stronger than that if you choose to go it alone, Miss Wilson."

She dropped the canvas flap in his face, then turned and hopped to the pallet on her crutches.

Still, his whisper managed to penetrate the heavy canvas. "You know what your problem is, Miss Wilson?"

No. Pray tell, Mr. Redlin. What is my problem? She remained silent, knowing full well she was going to find out soon enough.

He bent closer to the open slit. "You don't like men."

"I do so like men."

It came out much louder than she had intended. She turned to see both Sadie and Adele sit straight up on their pallets. They stared at her in the dim lantern light.

"Sorry," Copper murmured.

Adele yawned. "What's going on?"

"Just talking to myself. Go back to sleep."

"Lands," Sadie muttered, dropping back to her pillow. "Can you do it in a quieter tone?"

Chapter 9

The sun barely topped the rise as the women stood knee-deep in the stream, manning scrub boards. Restless with pain, Copper struggled with resentment. One day each week the wagons rested, always near water so the women could catch up on the laundry while men mended harnesses and did various other repair chores. If this was intended to be a day of rest, it looked to her like a lot of work was going on, and her pain wasn't getting any better.

This morning she sat at water's edge watching the work. The women scrubbed and wrung garments to later hang on lines fashioned between the wagons. Though last night's harmless excursion with Mike hadn't been mentioned, Copper knew the subject was uppermost in the women's minds. At first she wanted to deny that she'd acted improperly, but then she decided she had done nothing wrong and bringing it up would only suggest that she had. Redlin might think she was "cavorting," but nothing could be further from the truth. Yet very few women spoke to her this morning. They called back and forth, apparently enjoying their work, but giving her the silent treatment. Even Sadie had not been her usual cordial self.

"Hey, if you'll hand me some garments I'll be glad to wring them for you." She couldn't get into the water; she should help in some fashion.

Nodding, the women wordlessly began hurling wet shirts and pants at her. She ducked, surprised by the almost mean-spirited barrage, but she wasn't going to mention the velocity of that last petticoat.

She wrung a shirt and tossed it into a bucket. "That rain bank looks to be moving closer."

Adele paused, putting her wet hands on her hips. She scanned the approaching front. "Won't be here before evening. We'll have plenty of time to dry laundry." The women returned to their conversation on a particular stew recipe some swore by and others avoided.

After a while of the continuing snub Copper blurted, "I merely accompanied Mike when he took the mail to the post. If I'd known it would cause such a fuss I'd never have gone." She pitched a pair of denims in the container.

Scrubbing ceased. Eyes turned to center on her.

Copper felt heat creep up her neck. Why had she opened her big mouth? She didn't owe these people an apology. The world would not cease to spin on its axis because she accepted a simple moonlight excursion with a single young man.

Adele broke the strained silence. "Why, honey, why would you defend a moonlight walk with Mike? He's a fine boy—"

"He *isn't* courting me, Adele." How vain did they take her for? They didn't know her well enough to accuse her of chasing a man. The heat in her cheeks blazed. "Redlin said that some of you thought my actions objectionable."

"Hogwash." Adele picked up a pair of unmentionables and proceeded to scrub. "Sounds to me like the only objections come from him."

Sadie paused, wiping soap off her elbows. She focused on Copper. "Now wait a minute. I thought you weren't interested in Redlin."

"I'm not!" Copper denied.

"Leave her alone, Sadie." Nellie Fisher threw a man's shirt into her basket. "You know you have about as much chance of attracting Redlin as a snowball in you-know-where. That man's not going to suddenly wake up one morning and propose marriage to you."

"Nellie," Adele scolded, "that's a right uncharitable thing to say. You can't speak of Redlin's feelings."

"I don't know anything about the man other than he tends his own business, reads his Bible nightly, and I've never caught him mooning over Sadie or any other woman. You know the Nelsons have that young pretty daughter, and I've never seen Redlin say more than good morning or evening to her."

Sadie's crestfallen expression tugged at Copper's heartstrings. It was plain mean for Nellie to say such a thing. Sadie might not be every man's cup of tea, but she was good-hearted and she would give you the blouse off her back if she thought you needed it. Copper sprang to spare the woman's feelings. "Actually, I believe Mr. Redlin is already spoken for."

She immediately regretted the outburst. Work ceased. Women stood in the stream, wet garments dripping soapy water.

Sadie cocked her head. "What makes you say that?"

"Because I accidentally saw a letter he mailed last night."
Accidentally, her foot. She'd nearly broken her neck trying
to read the postmark, but the women didn't need to know
everything. Gossip was the devil's work, but Copper was
never sure where the line parted between gossip and fact,
and the fact was she'd seen a letter addressed to "Susan" in
Dallas.

Gossip, she supposed, was passing along such information,
but she was in too deep to back down now.

Sadie half waded to the bank. "So? All of us mail letters."

"But this letter was addressed to a woman in Dallas, and
granted I have no idea who the woman is, but it could mean
that he has someone waiting for him when he completes his
job."

Sadie fatalistically shook her head. "A wife."

"No—at least the last name wasn't the same."

Sadie's face screwed in concentration. "Sister?"

Copper shrugged, wishing she'd never mentioned the subject. She only did so to comfort Sadie but the woman looked
anything but relieved about the speculation. "Sadie? Have
you and Mr. Redlin courted?" Copper asked.

One or two women snickered and Copper shot them a
stern look. Sadie might be a little rough around the edges,
and she was anything but feminine by nature, but she was
a hard worker and loyal to a fault. One man had found
her worthy of marriage, and another would too. If not
Redlin— Well, granted, she had to admit as much as the
man annoyed her, he was a striking male with a smidgen
of appeal and a good deal of empathy. She supposed that
came from all the Bible reading he did. The man knew
Scripture. He asked grace over the evening meals and

talked to the Maker with such ease and familiarity that Copper could vow that somewhere in his past he had a history of religious service.

"I only mentioned the letter for all of our benefits." She nearly choked, but she continued. "It would be difficult for any woman to deny that the wagon master has certain . . . undeniable appeal." She glanced at Sadie. "So no one should feel badly if the man has a private life that he's chosen not to reveal. And that life might well include a woman—a fiancée—a . . ." She wanted to say *donkey with a similar personality* but she refrained. She only wanted to dampen Sadie's hopes, not to dash her dreams. "A Susan."

"Copper's right, you know." Adele reached for a dishcloth. "Redlin keeps his private life to himself. His job is to get us to Colorado Springs, but otherwise I guess the man has a right to a personal life."

Others agreed. Even Sadie nodded, and Copper sagged with relief. She had no idea about Josh Redlin's personal life—and she didn't want to know. But she hoped she had somewhat dashed Sadie's unrealistic expectations for the man. Truthfully, as much as she liked Sadie, she couldn't, in her wildest dreams, imagine Josh and her together. She had a feeling Josh was wanting a nice, submissive woman, and Sadie didn't fit that description. Sadie was more like . . . her. Spirited. Able to hold her own with the opposite sex.

Shortly after noon, with the school lesson finished and laundry flapping on the line, Copper stretched out on a blanket to read a copy of *A Fairy Tale* by Louisa M. Alcott. Reading took her to new worlds, and today she felt in need of distraction.

A commotion caught her attention and she glanced up to see four braves ride into camp. Pulse quickening, she thought of the children.

Please God, let them remember our lesson on fear, and please let this be an "irrational one."

Men with rifles in hands stood well back as Josh and Frank Richardson approached the small party. Copper figured the braves couldn't be looking for trouble with the relay station and soldiers close by.

The men engaged in conversation. From her vantage point, Copper couldn't hear the exchange but it appeared to be expressed in nonthreatening tones. Suddenly her heart hammered so forcefully she thought it would break through the chest wall. What if the redskins decided to turn on the two men?

In a second they could be dead with an arrow through the heart before others could fire.

She eased closer to the edge of the pallet, wishing for a gun. She could shoot. She was not an expert, but if one of those savages decided to go after Redlin she felt sure she could put a round within a few inches of the intended target.

The small party conversed another few minutes, and then the braves turned their ponies and rode toward the chuck wagon.

The camp guards dispersed, their concerns apparently eased.

Reaching for her crutches, Copper awkwardly got to her feet and approached Josh, who was coming back to camp with Frank Richardson.

Redlin acknowledged her with a nod of the head when she

met him at the end of the wagon. "Something I can do for you, Miss Wilson?"

"Please stop with the Miss Wilson. I think we know each other well enough to speak our given names."

"What'd you need, Copper?"

She inclined her head toward the prior meeting spot. "What was that about?"

He turned to look where she indicated, and then turned back. "The braves?"

She sighed. "No, the grass. Of course the braves! What did they want?"

"Think I'll just leave you two to duke it out." Frank Richardson tipped his brim and walked on, chuckling under his breath.

Removing his hat, Josh ran a hand through his hair. "They wanted to herd our stock tonight."

"Herd our stock?"

"They say they know of good pasture up the road."

"And you'd trust them to take our stock?"

"No. I would send Mike and Doug with them, but yes, I hired them to take the stock for the night. They'll have it back by sunup."

"Won't they be armed? How can you believe them?"

His tolerant look was enough to bring color to her cheeks. "I give you my word, they won't be armed, but Mike and Doug will be. The stock hasn't had good pasture in a few days so I took them up on their offer. It's common practice so don't worry your pretty head about it."

Copper's eyes shifted to the chuck wagon where the braves were now off their ponies. "Are you going to feed them too?"

"Super and breakfast—that's all they want."

"There's four of them. You're going to send all four?"

"No, two will ride ahead until they find another train and offer the same service—why all of the interest? Are you running this train now?" He grinned. "Didn't I hear you explaining fear and irrational fear to the kids the other day?"

"Yes . . ." She bit down on her lower lip. "And I regret the lesson. I wanted to make an impression, and now I fear I might have made them lax. One asked how I could tell if their fears were rational or irrational, and I didn't have an answer."

He reached out and tweaked her nose. "If you find an arrow in your back, they're rational."

When she didn't smile, he sobered. "There isn't an answer. You use caution, but eventually you get to know their habits and you can pretty well figure out their sense of purpose. If you're going to make a mistake, make it on the side of caution, if that helps."

They turned and she kept pace with him.

"I also bought four sides of antelope from them," he said. "Thought the folks might enjoy some fresh meat tonight."

As much as she hated to admit it, the man could be pleasant when he wanted, and today he wanted. He treated his job with respect, and the folks in his party like family.

He nodded toward the crutch. "How's the ankle?"

"Very painful."

His gaze softened. "We'll be in Fort Riceson soon." She noticed he didn't try to annoy her with anxious thoughts of flooded rivers and broken wheels. His answer was as close to real information as she'd come, and she was relieved to hear the journey would soon be over.

"I'm frightened." For the first time, she felt herself opening to him. "If I allow myself to think about the possibility of—"

He interrupted. "Dyson is the best. I had heard of his work before you were injured. If the ankle can be fixed, he'll do it. If not, then you live with what God gives you."

Resentment built in the back of her mind. "That's easy to say when you're not the one with trouble. You've never had to experience anything like this."

He chuckled but not with mirth.

She glanced over, perplexed. "What?"

"Do you think you're the only person on earth with problems?"

"No, but—"

"You're not." He answered for her. "You've got a heavy load, I'll grant you that, but whatever happens, you'll make it through."

"How can you be so certain? You hardly know me."

"Because I know people, and I know you well enough to say you've got what it takes to make it through this world."

She wished she felt as confident as he sounded.

"That was a compliment, Miss Wilson."

She glanced over and grinned. "I know. Was that so hard?"

He shrugged. "Took all I had, but I got it out."

By now they'd reached Adele's wagon. They paused, and he removed his hat. "The thing I said about accepting whatever God sends your way? I still have to work on that one myself. It's not easy, and it takes a powerful lot of thinking to not resent God during the hard times."

She couldn't believe her ears. The man who had once

grated on her nerves beyond anything she'd experienced, was now talking to her seriously, and sharing some of the struggles he faced. She'd always imagined having these kinds of conversation with a man, but never thought it would be Josh.

"Thank you, and thank you for the vote of confidence."

He turned to leave, and then slowly turned back. "Regretfully, I hate to ruin the mood, but I have something I need to say and I don't want you flying off the handle. Agreed?"

She stiffened. And they were getting along so well. "What?"

"Agreed?"

"Agreed—within limits."

"Don't be spreading any more rumors or speculations about my correspondence."

She was quite certain that if a face could physically hit the ground, hers would have at that moment. "Why . . . I . . ." She was sputtering and she knew it. Who'd told on her? Nellie? Well, woe to her if she ever mentioned another word around that nosy body.

"Look." His tone gentled even more. "I'm not getting on you, I'm just asking that you don't be speculating about things you know nothing about. Do we have an agreement?"

She nodded, embarrassed speechless. Mortified. He was right. She'd had no call to theorize about his personal life.

"Hey." He tilted her chin to meet his gaze. "I'm not angry with you. I just happen to be a private man who doesn't like speculation. Rumors can turn ugly and mean and innocent folks can get hurt."

"I'm sorry," she murmured. "Of course you're right, and I was out of place." It would be of no value to explain her motive, though chances were Josh knew Sadie's expectations and had decided long ago to ignore the matter.

Why hadn't she been as wise?

That night the rain moved in. Copper lay on her pallet listening first to the thunder and lightning, and then the downpour as it lashed the canvas. For some reason the laudanum was not easing the pain much this time, and she prayed for the hazy spell the drug normally produced.

Her thoughts drifted to Josh Redlin. He wasn't so bad—good conversationalist, knowledgeable, and he certainly knew his job. The antelope had made a wonderful supper, and later some men had taken the remains to the way station to share among the soldiers.

All in all, it had been a good day—maybe even a fine day. Soon she would know her fate, and as Josh had said, she was strong, strong enough to accept whatever God sent her way.

She only wished she was as certain of her inner strength as he seemed to be.

Chapter 10

Heavy rain couldn't disguise the sound of bawling cattle and braying jackasses.

An hour before dawn, the mules woke the whole camp. Sitting up, Copper blinked back sleep, trying to focus.

Adele rolled to her side and pulled the blanket over her head. "Stock's back."

Falling back to her pillow, Copper sighed. All that worry over nothing. When would she learn to trust Josh's word? He hadn't been wrong yet.

Breakfast was last night's fare. The travelers huddled against a blowing rain and ate in silence. Redlin led the daily devotions, and compared travel ordeals to the Israelites wandering in the wilderness. He pointed out that their forty-year wanderings were due to the fact that they had disobeyed God, but that in his love he continued to provide manna and quail for them anyway. Though conditions weren't ideal, God would provide the needed strength to reach their destination if they kept the faith.

Services ended, and the travelers headed to their rigs. At exactly eight o'clock, the party pulled out. The back wheels of Adele's wagons were stuck and it took her and Sadie and three other good-sized men ten minutes to break the rig loose and catch up.

Copper waved to the post soldiers as the prairie schooners and Conestogas rumbled past. Mike and Doug rode ahead of Redlin and Richardson. They would decide the campground for that night.

"Sort of reminds me of Thunder Ridge," Adele called above the creaking of rotating wheels and pouring rain.

Copper nodded. Her thoughts were also with Willow and Audrey. They would be dressing for church services, decked in their best. Reverend Cordell would preach, Willow would play the new organ, and then they'd go home to a hot dinner of fried chicken and cornbread. Homesickness swept through her like an ice storm. She shuddered.

Adele glanced over. "Cold?"

Last night's weather front brought not only rain, but a bone-rattling wind. It was a miserable time to be traveling. She huddled deeper into the warm blanket wrapped around her shoulders. "No, just homesick."

"A terrible thing." Adele clucked to the team. "Just know that family and friends are thinking of you too."

Remembering wasn't the problem; memories were the source of her misery.

Noon meal was eaten in wagons. Rain fell in buckets, and Copper had sent word down the line there'd be no lesson today.

Late afternoon, she slipped into a slicker and eased up front to sit on the driver's bench and visit with Sadie, who now manned the two-horse team. Some rigs had four animals; some had only two to pull the load. Adele had mentioned that this train had stock problems. Many families started out with a two-horse team and a wagon too heavily loaded. Long before the train had reached Thunder Ridge many had been forced to jettison furniture and other heavy objects. Adele said that if the trail got really muddy Redlin would have to temporarily hitch part of his stock to some of the wagons to help keep the train moving.

That afternoon, Copper turned on her seat to peer back at the terrain. Today their rig was one of the last because of their late start.

"That's the third time you've craned your neck like that. What are you looking for? Indians?"

"No. There's another wagon train following us. Has been all day."

Sadie whistled to the team. "I've had my eye on 'em."

"Who are they?" And why were they following so close? Soldiers had stopped Redlin's train a couple of times and asked him to add a small group of travelers. In Indian country there was safety in numbers and the military would not allow a small train to travel alone. He had never been pleased with the arrangement, but he was not willing to contribute to the death of any of them. Besides, the soldiers had not really given him any choice. And, so far, none of the newcomers had been any trouble, the train was just getting bigger.

"Don't know. They must know where the checkpoints are and they're avoiding them. Not a smart thing to do."

"Why *would* anyone do that? Aren't they concerned about their welfare?"

She shrugged. "Folks are strange. Some don't want to bother with guard duty or the discipline of a larger group."

Independent. Do as they pleased. Copper related, but this trip had changed her mind about self-reliance. Independence was a good thing, but having your scalp still attached at the end of the day was better. She reached for the notepad she kept handy and jotted down thoughts for future lessons.

By late afternoon the rain let up and a cold sun peeked out while they were making camp. Most ate and went straight to bed, plain worn out from fighting the elements all day.

Copper wrote in her journal about the date's events, and the strange wagon train following so close. It seemed the laudanum was taking longer and longer to work each evening.

Haven't seen much of Redlin today. He rode a ways up, while our wagon traveled near the back. I suppose I should be thankful he wasn't around to infuriate me, but oddly enough I missed the distraction. I thought I might catch him at supper but someone said he was bandaging a mule's ankle. Lucky mule . . .

She hurriedly struck the last thought.

The weather evened out, and by mid-morning the following day Copper peeled out of her heavy shawl. The sycamores and cottonwoods were turning brown. Overnight, it seemed, the rain and cooler temperatures had started the annual fall ritual. She remembered God's promise to Noah after the flood that the seasons of the year would never cease. It seemed a little sad that the leaves reached their greatest glory only in their death.

She whirled when Redlin rode up beside their wagon. Tipping his hat, he smiled. "Morning, ladies."

Sadie broke into a wreath of smiles. "Morning, Redlin."

Josh's eye skimmed Copper. "How are you this fine day?"

"Breathing, thank you. Are we nearly there?"

"Yep." He winked. "We ford the river tomorrow, and Fort Riceson's another day's ride." Assessing the blue sky, he smiled. "Looks like the rain is over." Kicking the horse into a gallop, he rode away before she could ask him if he'd noticed they had company. Four wagons following half a mile behind.

"Sadie? You think he knows about those wagons?"

Sadie laughed. "He knows."

"Did you tell him?"

She shook her head. "No ma'am, don't need to. He knows."

Copper hoped that she knew what she was talking about. She knew nothing about wagon travel other than what she'd recently encountered, but she was sure that four unidentified wagons following on their heels could spell trouble.

Maybe big trouble.

After supper, Copper made her way to the creek where the men were shooting. She moved far enough downstream to take a brisk sponge bath before she emerged from the willows growing along the bank. Thankfully, the shooting session was over and the men were packing up to leave. She approached Josh as he picked up the Henry and a double-barrel shotgun and started off.

"Josh?"

He turned. "Yes?"

"May I have a word?"

He reversed his steps and approached. "What can I do for you?"

"There are four wagons following us—have been for the past two days."

He nodded.

"You've seen them?"

He indicated a fallen log. "Sit down."

"I don't want to sit. I've been sitting all day."

"Don't make me pick you up and put you on that log. I've had a long day, and I'm in no mood to argue."

She sank to the log.

Propping the guns on a nearby stump, he then sat down beside her, answering her question. "I don't know who they are. I thought they might break away sometime today and travel in a different direction, but so far they haven't. The river's up some from the heavy rain; could be they're hanging around, hoping to cross with us."

"Well, that hardly seems fair. Crossing with us would mean managing four more wagons and their stock, which seems to be plentiful. And more important, extra wagons would only slow us more."

"I'm going to talk to them before we pull out in the morning."

"Talk indeed. You order them to stay back, observe proper etiquette." The very nerve of people, crowding in where they weren't invited.

"Yes. I'll be sure and use those exact words."

She glanced over, ignoring his jest. "You will not. You have no trouble speaking your mind with me, but when it comes to others you're too courteous. I'll go with you."

He shook his head, looking away, but it was only too clear that he agreed because he was laughing at her. She could see his shoulders heave.

She narrowed her eyes.

He threw up his hands. "Okay, I'll be a barbarian. I'll ride in with guns blazing and arrows flying. I'll scalp a couple of women, shoot a few horses, and prove that I mean business."

He would do no such thing. He would ask them their business, and then ask them to keep proper distance from his train. If those folks were bold enough to follow for two days, his words would fall on deaf ears. "I'm going with you."

He sobered. "You are not."

"Yes I am. I know you. You'll be all nicety nice and they'll still be following us in the morning, and when we get to the river you'll feel obligated to let them cross with us, which, may I remind you, will delay us for who knows how long? We added two more wagons at the last checkpoint." She altered her tone to civil when she realized her objection had turned stringent. "Don't you care that I'm in awful pain, and if we dally too long I might suffer permanent consequences of your error in judgment?"

He reached over and traced a finger along her jawline, then touched her cheek. His gaze softened. "Of course I care. I know you put up a good front, but Adele keeps me informed on your condition. I know that you're never out of pain, that the medicine takes longer to work now. I know about the night sweats and the nightmares, and I know about your fears. I'm doing the best I can to get you to the fort as quickly as I can. We're close. Just hang on for another few days and trust me."

She blinked back tears. She hated it when he was kind. It made her like him, really like him. And she didn't want to like him, didn't want to consider the sort of upheaval that such a "like" might add to her life. Somewhere a woman in Dallas named Susan waited for him. Was she important to him—important in a forever kind of way? She had no way of knowing, and why would she entertain the idea that her feelings would matter to Redlin? He was all man, and she could very likely be a cripple the rest of her life. Every moment's delay brought her closer to that very real possibility, and what man would want a cripple for . . . She couldn't finish the senseless thought.

"I'm going with you," she repeated in a tone far more docile than her intentions. Nobody told Redlin what to do; not even Copper Wilson. But she decided she could have Sadie or Adele saddle a horse and take her to the trailing wagons if Redlin refused. She would get up before sunrise and be there and back before Josh rolled out of bed. After all, it was her welfare at stake, not his.

Josh met her defiant look. "You're not going. Richardson will ride out with me. We don't know who's in those wagons or their purpose."

"I'm going. Like I said, you won't be firm enough. I'll show them my ankle, and if they're decent folk they'll know we don't have time to get them across the river. They'll just have to wait their turn to join up with another train. Apparently they've decided to avoid the military and travel alone, so they'll have to face the consequences of their actions."

A muscle worked in his jaw. "We don't know their purpose, and you're not going."

She took a deep breath. "The only way you can stop me is to shoot the horse out from under me, and you wouldn't do that to good stock." She'd seen him with animals. She remembered how he had treated a jackass's ankle when most men would have disposed of the animal.

"Don't be so sure. I might not value the animal if something or someone is on it, refusing to listen to me."

She sighed and reached for the crutches. "Good evening, Mr. Redlin."

"Sleep tight, Miss Wilson. And bury this thought in your mind. Deep. You're not to go near those wagons."

Let him think what he liked. He wasn't about to become a cripple. He didn't live with the pain day in and day out.

Come morning, she was getting to those wagons if she had to crawl.

Chapter 11

"Sadie, you *have* to take me." The sun wasn't up and Sadie refused to budge.

"No ma'am, I don't have to do anything but answer to the good Lord on Judgment Day, drive this wagon, and keep my nose out of other folks' business. It's a long way to Colorado, and I don't intend to be thrown off this train because you and Redlin butt heads."

Copper turned to Adele.

The older woman shook her head. "Same goes for me, young'un. You know if I could I'd help, but I'm getting old and I shore can't walk to Colorado. Besides, the last thing you need to be doing is cavorting around the countryside on horseback."

"Fine." Copper reached for her crutches. "Traitors."

"You ain't near as pretty when you're in this mood," Adele advised, and proceeded to make her bed. "But I will loan you some britches if you got your heart set on aggravating Josh this early in the morning. Can't ride a horse in a dress and with that ankle."

Copper had to admit that further antagonizing Redlin wasn't the smartest idea, but those four wagons sorely grated on her. She was so close to relief. Only one obstacle now stood in her way: the river. After that, help was close by.

Dressed in Adele's old trousers and a shirt, she eased from the wagon and spotted the young Irish lad hitching a team. Copper called out, "Mike!"

He glanced up. "Yes ma'am?"

Copper made it to the wagon, breathless. "I have a favor to ask." Her gaze scanned the area for Redlin. Richardson was standing beside the fire drinking coffee. Good. The men hadn't left yet.

"Sure thing." The boy dropped a harness and approached. "What can I do for you?"

"Would you saddle a horse for me?"

Confusion flickered in his eyes. "A horse?"

"Something small—a mare."

"What for, Miss Wilson? If you need to go somewhere I'll take you. We won't be pulling out for a while."

"Thank you, Mike, but I'd just enjoy an early ride—a brief trot around the corral to stir the blood?"

Flashing a grin, he nodded. "Sitting gets pretty old, eh?"

"Aye. Real tiresome." She wasn't fibbing—exactly. Sitting did get old, and she could think of nothing more enjoyable on this morning than a ride through the foggy haze.

Within minutes he'd saddled a horse and led it to her. Lifting her into the saddle, he warned, "You take care. This one's gentle, but we don't need for you to aggravate that ankle."

She wouldn't. She kept her aggravation for Redlin. "Thank you, Mike, but don't worry. I've been riding horses all of my life." She reined the animal, and the mare trotted around the corral with a steady, easy gait. Completing a second turn, she called, "I'm taking her out a little farther!"

She wasn't going to lie to accomplish her purpose. She just didn't intend to say how far outside the camp.

Mike nodded, waving her on.

Kneeing the horse, she set the animal into an easy gallop through the gate opening. Her heart kept rhythm with the pounding hooves, feeling lighter than she'd felt in months. The brisk predawn air loosened her hair, and tendrils whipped her face. She'd forgotten how freedom felt, how it felt to be one with the animal. Urgency filled her now. She had to reach the wagons before Redlin, and state her case. She'd be polite but resolved. Those wagons must allow the Redlin party to cross the river and reach the fort before their party followed.

She galloped the mare to within a short distance of the intruders and reined up. The pain from her ankle was more than she had expected, but it was secondary to the urgency of her mission. Nothing stirred. She glanced at the sky, dark with gathering rain clouds. Drat the weather. The last thing they needed was more rain.

Her gaze scanned the quietness. Nobody was up. Perhaps that meant they planned to stay in camp today. Her spirits rose. There wouldn't be a confrontation; the Redlin party would be pulling out early and these folks would still be abed. But—and this thought elated her more than the party's laziness—she'd beat Josh at his game.

Wheeling the horse, she came face to face with her adversary. A grim-faced Frank Richardson sat beside Redlin. Both men looked anything but happy to see her.

Looking away, the wagon master apparently reined his anger before he turned back. "Miss Wilson."

She nodded. "Mr. Redlin."

"I see you're up and about early this morning."

She braced for the explosion that oddly enough failed to come.

Inclining his head toward the four wagons, he asked, "Is anybody home?"

"I'm not sure." Copper turned to trace the men's eyes. "I assume they're all still sleeping."

Her mare snuffed, shaking its mane.

Strained silence settled over the three riders. Finally Josh kneed his horse forward, and Richardson and Copper fell in behind. As they approached the camp, Josh called out, "Friend!"

A man's voice came back. "Over here!"

The animals rounded the lead wagon, and Copper spotted a well-dressed gentleman standing in front of the fire holding a cup of coffee. The bone china cup and saucer caught her attention: flow blue pattern, and exquisite.

The man frowned, curiosity etched in his aristocratic features. "May I help you?"

Copper eased forward in the saddle, ready to argue her case, but Josh's strident glance rendered her speechless.

"Name's Redlin. I'm head of the party in front of you."

"Oh yes." The man extended a hand. "Reginald Newsome, from Shreveport. What can I do for you?"

"Noticed you folks have been following us pretty close for the past few days."

"Following you?" The man shook his head and sipped from his cup. "I believe this is a public road. One does occasionally have to follow other wagons if they're headed in the same direction."

Josh remained pleasant. "You're right, but I thought you might like to join up with us. We'd be glad to have the extra hands."

Join up? Copper seethed. She knew he'd do something like this. Join up indeed! They needed to drop back. Way back.

"No, there's only the two wagons. We're doing fine."

Copper's eyes focused on four wagons.

"Two?" Josh's gaze followed hers. "One of us can't count."

"Only two containing my family and myself. The other two contain supplies." He bent closer, whispering. "I have a young daughter. She requires more—er—room, shall we say? The remaining two wagons hold her clothing and frivolities. You know women."

A black woman appeared, carrying a supply box. She bent and set to work frying bacon.

Josh met the man's direct gaze. "You're aware that it's wise to travel with a larger train."

"Yes. So they say, but we prefer to do it our way. We haven't spotted an Indian, and as you can see"—he flashed an indulgent smile—"we prefer to sleep late and get a tardier start than you people."

Yet they were always half a mile behind their train. Copper bit her lip, determined to let Josh handle the situation. She wouldn't step in unless forced to, and this elite snob, though naive, appeared harmless.

Josh smiled. "Want to invite you again to join us. River's

coming up, and more rain will likely have it out of its banks. It'll be hard to move your wagons across with so little help."

"There's a river coming up?"

Richardson glanced at Redlin.

"Buffalo. Be coming to it soon. When it's out of its banks, it's hard to cross."

"Well, you needn't be concerned for our welfare, but we thank you for the invitation. My girls." He inclined his head to the lead wagon, where all was quiet. "They abhor rules and regulations, and quite frankly, they've spoiled me. I don't like guard duty." He chuckled and lifted his cup to sip. "I'm afraid I've grown quite slothful in my waning years."

Josh reined his horse around. "If you change your mind let us know. Otherwise, keep your wagons back a day or two from ours."

"A day or two?" Reginald's features sobered. "I think not. This is a public roadway. You don't own it."

"No sir, I don't, but neither do you, and in these parts there's no law except the ones we make for ourselves, and I'm telling you to keep your wagons back two days from ours."

He visibly stiffened. "I shall not. You have no call to ask such a thing."

"Then join up with us, do your share of work, and we'll help you ford the river."

"I'll do no such thing."

A young woman parted the back canvas and peered out, blinking sleep from her round blue eyes. Copper took note of her stunning beauty. She wasn't much younger than Copper, but her porcelain skin, blond hair, and stunning shade of ocean-blue eyes could turn any man's head. Glancing at Josh, she noticed he hadn't missed the sight. She glanced at her hands, red and rough from hours of washing clothes in a cold stream. She quickly stuffed them into her pockets. And she hadn't bothered to comb her hair this morning.

"Daddy!" the daughter complained. "It's so early! You woke me."

"Sorry, Pudding." He turned accusing eyes on the Redlin party. "Now you've wakened Milly."

The flap dropped back into place and Reginald lowered his tone. "I believe our business is concluded. We shall not join your train nor shall we keep our wagon two days back. We're not accountable to you, and I would appreciate it if you'd ride out. Milly and Florence are trying to sleep."

Copper couldn't hold her tongue another moment. "If you intend to keep up with our wagons, how can you sleep this late?" Redlin pulls out at eight o'clock sharp."

The man lifted his nose. "Our niggers take care of the mundane. The women sleep as long as they're so inclined."

Copper had to bite her lip to keep from lashing out at the man like a coiled rattler. Indeed. She had helped fight a war over the attitudes inherent in that ugly term. Men like Reginald Newsome should be strung up and horsewhipped.

"Miss Wilson," Josh softly warned.

She drew a deep breath and clamped down on her tongue.

He nodded. "Like the man said, our business is over." Reining the mare, Copper fell in behind Richardson and Redlin and the three galloped out.

"Mean enough for you?" Josh asked Copper on the ride back to camp.

"You were a kitten—a meek little kitten. He's a thoughtless, vile snob. But I suppose he got the message."

"That's what you think."

She glanced over. "Don't you think you made your point?"

Redlin shrugged. "We understand each other."

"Well, at least we won't be delayed," Copper said. "You say the fort is within a day's ride once we cross the river?"

Josh nodded. "We're nearly there."

The three horses galloped into camp, and Mike ran out to meet them. "I was about to ride out looking for you."

Copper handed him the reins. "Why? I had a splendid ride, and I haven't been gone long."

"Just splendid," Josh mocked her.

Mike's young features closed. "We got big trouble." The urgency in his tone turned heads.

Josh frowned. "What's wrong?"

"The Sniders' toddler. She wandered out of camp half an hour ago. We've been searching everywhere but we can't find the little girl anywhere." Mike paused. "And she's not wearing shoes."

Chapter 12

Fourteen-month-old Carrie Snider had walked barefoot away from her wagon and disappeared. A lost child struck terror in the hearts of all fathers and mothers, and the weather had turned mean. Rigging and teams were forgotten as almost everyone spread out to search for the girl. Those that remained with the wagons formed a supportive cluster around the hysterical mother.

Against everyone's wishes, Copper insisted on participating in the search. With all the confusion she barely noticed the pain in her ankle. She was aboard the mare, and no one, not even Redlin, was going to talk her out of looking for that baby.

When full daylight arrived a cool west wind blew through the camp. The baby was shoeless on a windy, overcast day. The thought of the darling cherub, with her sunny disposition and chubby cheeks, drove Copper farther and farther away from the circle of wagons. Three men rode with her, friends from neighboring rigs. Grim-faced men scanned every bush, rain-swollen ditch, and creek.

The party passed the Louisiana wagons that strangely enough were now hitched and awaiting departure. Only the thought of the lost child prevented Copper from stopping long enough to give those folks a tongue-lashing they would not soon forget.

An hour passed, then a second. Threatening clouds roiled overhead. A sense of urgency was present in the faces of each of the searchers.

By mid-morning, Copper could no longer ignore the torture radiating from her ankle. Her foot was puffy inside her bandage, yet she refused to give in to the agony. She could sit in camp and help comfort Lil Snider, but her nature wouldn't permit it. Children were God's gift. She was gaining a better understanding of why she had chosen to teach young minds. She'd come from an affluent family, her papa from a line of "old money" as some were known to say. She had been given two choices: Choose any man within her realm of society or (to her socialite mother's chagrin) further her education. She chose the latter. She'd been told that she was a gifted student, completing her early education by the time she was fifteen. Papa and Mother had turned absolutely green when she informed them that she wanted to move to Texas and teach, but Papa had never denied his only child a single thing. Only now was she starting to realize that perhaps through her parents' love and complete devotion, Mama had raised a selfish daughter and Papa had created a self-centered individual.

During noon hour, the clouds opened and the rain began again. Not a single sign of the missing child had been found.

Not a lost bonnet, a strip of torn dress, or the rag doll the child carried constantly.

Richardson insisted that the mother be given something from the train's medicine box to calm her. The young woman's collapse was hard to witness, but if the child wasn't found soon the mother would be inconsolable. She tossed fitfully on a pallet in her wagon while the distraught husband searched or paced back and forth in front of the wagon.

"You shouldn't be doing this, Miss Wilson." Mike helped her back aboard the mare and settled her injured foot in the stirrup.

"Don't fuss at me, Mike. You know I can't sit by and watch. I need to be doing something."

"Just don't ride off on your own," he warned. "I haven't seen an Indian but they're out there."

Yes, they were out there, and the thought haunted every member of the search party. Little Carrie would make a fine Comanche trophy, or a thoughtful gift for a childless mother. She nudged the horse to catch up with the rest of her group.

Mid-afternoon her party caught up with Redlin's group. The searchers paused in a willow stand, their horses blowing white breath in the falling temperatures.

A man from Copper's party said, "We've searched every inch of the area, Josh. She's nowhere to be found."

Redlin nodded, openly confirming everyone's unspoken fear. "We've covered it well. She could have fallen into the stream. With this rain, the current would have swept her downstream."

Copper's heart caught in her throat. The woman riding beside her turned her head away.

Redlin glanced at the sky. "We have a couple hours before dark. You take the riverbank leading north and we'll take the south bank." He pulled the brim of his hat lower. "Be back in camp an hour before dark."

Copper protested. "But we can't just leave the child out here."

Josh reined his horse. "An hour before dark." Nudging the animal, he rode off, and his party fell in behind him.

Copper's group rode the south bank. Occasionally the searchers would form a huddle and one or the other men led them in prayer. "God, we need your help" sounded so many times, the phrase echoed over and over in Copper's mind. The huddle would break up, and the riders would continue the search down the bank. Rain thrummed the ground and the small stream swelled to new heights.

An hour before dark, Richardson reined up. He faced the weary riders, and Copper wondered if she had ever seen such raw emotion on any man's face. "We're due back."

Some argued; to leave the child out on a night like this would be a certain death sentence.

Richardson was so much like Josh that it both broke and strengthened her heart. Someone had to be strong. Someone had to say when to stop, and the agony of leadership was imprinted on the faces of both men.

Quietly turning their animals, the small party rode back to camp. As they galloped past the four wagons, Copper noted they'd waited. The Negro slave bent in the steady rain to coax the fire where fat slabs of beef struggled to sizzle.

After supper, Josh led a prayer service for Carrie Snider. Copper's heart ached when he asked for comfort for the grieving mother and father. Every person in the group knew that when the train pulled out in the morning, the little girl was lost forever. Prayerful vigil had not produced results.

"How can this be?" a distraught mother called softly from the sidelines when Josh admitted that he didn't always, if ever, understand the ways of the Lord. But he stated again, with an air of certainty that seemed almost cruel under the circumstances, that he only understood that they were to trust and accept, regardless of how painful the situation.

He shook his head, rain dripping from the brim of his hat. It was as though the angels were crying tonight. "I wish I knew the answer, Mrs. Bellows. Good Lord knows I wish I knew."

Copper wiped her eyes, recalling the way the toddler was always hungry. She seemed a bottomless pit, always asking, "Num, num," her word for *hungry*. And she loved books. Oh, how she loved books. No matter how many times *Mr. Bear and the Moon* had been read to her, she always wanted to hear it again.

Talk quietly centered on erecting a small marker in the toddler's name before the train pulled out the next morning.

Josh ended the service with a prayer for trust and guidance, and then asked that every man present stay for a brief meeting afterward.

The women departed, heading for dry wagons, while the men gathered in the center of the corral. Adele's rig was parked directly in front of the meeting place, so when Copper stepped upon the box into the wagon she could hear the men's conversation.

Redlin spoke. "You've all noticed the wagons following us?"

"Yes, what's that about," a fellow asked.

"I had a talk with them this morning. A man, his wife and daughter, and some slaves. Seems they hail from Shreveport, and I didn't ask where they were heading. They don't like rules and regulations. I invited them to join up, but they prefer to remain on their own. We'll be coming to the river soon. The question is this; do we help them across or let them fend for themselves?"

"How are they going to get four wagons across a river? This rain will have the water roiling by morning."

Josh again. "That's the purpose of this meeting. They won't get across, not without help."

"One family? Why four wagons?"

"I understand a couple of them hold supplies and the daughter's dresses and furniture."

Copper could imagine the men's reactions. Adele and Sadie were sitting with Carrie's mother, so she had the wagon to herself. She drew the curtain to block the light, and began to unbutton her rain-soaked dress, ear still tuned to the men's exchange.

"What's our choice?" someone asked.

"We can help or we can move on and let them go it alone."

"You invited them to join up?"

"Twice. Left the invitation open, but I told them if they don't join up they need to stay two days ride behind us."

"They weren't planning on that this morning. Their wagons were hitched and ready to roll when we rode out looking for the girl," Richardson said.

"I say we take a vote," a gruff voice called.

Redlin's voice followed. "All those in favor of helping when we come to the river, call out."

Dead silence followed.

"Those who want to grant their wish and let them go it alone?"

The *ayes* rattled Adele's wagon. Copper slipped into a warm nightgown, proud of their stance. Stupidity bothered her, and the Newsomes had a terminal case. She didn't wish the family harm, but they'd been given a choice and refused help. She'd have to hand it to Josh. He had handled the situation with empathy but with strength and wise judgment. She would have started a war if she'd been left to deal with the high-and-mighty family.

The Newsomes had chosen unwisely. Somewhere in the Good Book it said, "The fear of the Lord is the beginning of wisdom," and that family seemed not to have any of either. And the servants. Had Newsome given them a choice to leave, or had he failed to mention that the war was over, and slavery was abolished.

She hopped to her pallet, wincing when she encountered a smattering of soda cracker crumbs on the wagon floor. *Adele.* She had the messiest eating habits. Copper brushed away crumbs, too weary to sweep up. It could wait until morning.

Outside, the crowd dispersed. Several of the women, including Adele and Sadie, were still with an inconsolable Lil Snider. Copper had spotted Carrie's father sitting beside the wagon, coiled fists to his eyes.

Sighing, she dropped the laudanum under her tongue, and then blew out the light. Not only had this been the most tragic period of her life, they'd lost yet another day's travel. It seemed God didn't want her to reach the fort.

Crawling beneath cold sheets, she stretched out, and then suddenly froze. With a yelp, she rolled to the wagon floor and sucked in her breath when the injured foot struck the end of Adele's rocker. The pain reminded her of the abuse she had forced on her ankle all day.

Something was in her bed. Something rather large. And foreign.

Snake? Her heart hammered, and logic sat in. How would a snake get into her pallet? A snake would not be warm!

With trembling fingers, she struck a match and relit the lamp and then cautiously eased the blanket aside.

Carrie sat up, blinking her eyes.

Copper sagged with relief. Easing to her knees, she smothered the toddler with a bear hug, delirious with relief. "Where have you been, sweetie? Your parents have been looking for you all day!" Hadn't the child heard them calling. Shouting? If she had, she had chosen to ignore the summons.

The little girl, still drowsy from sleep, blinked innocently. "Weed."

Weed. Weed? Read! Copper spotted the mound of books. *Mr. Bear and the Moon* was lying on top. The child had attended every noon school session, and books fascinated her. Somehow she had climbed on top of the box step after Adele and Sadie left, into the wagon, and had spent the entire day huddled on the bed looking through the picture books or napping. Everyone was so preoccupied with the search or tending the stricken parents, they hadn't thought to thoroughly search the wagons.

The little girl said, "Num, num."

"You're hungry? Of course you are!" Copper recalled the patch of crumbs that she'd blamed on Adele. With only soda crackers to eat all day, the child must be thirsty and famished.

"Stay right here, sweetheart. I'll be right back."

Copper hopped through the pile of cracker crumbs and parted the back canvas. "Hey everybody! I have a hungry little girl in here!"

If Copper had ever once doubted that there was a God, he'd shown himself tonight.

Chapter 13

⌒

For some reason when the train pulled out the next morning, Copper was ruminating not on the Newsomes, who were still following, but on angels. Despite the answered prayers of finding the lost child, it seemed the angels were still weeping. Of course, now they were weeping for joy. Not that angels, as far as she knew, had human emotions. Nor would they need them to fulfill their role as God's messengers. With Carrie tucked safely in her folks' wagon, the rain did not seem nearly so menacing.

"Guess the old saying doesn't hold true," Copper remarked.

Adele maneuvered the wagon into line. "What saying, honey?"

"About when it's raining the angels are crying. Nobody in this train is sad this morning." Only relief and prayerful gratitude filled this party. Little Carrie was firmly enthroned on Lil's lap, cradled by a strong right arm. Last night's celebration had lasted well into the evening, and this morning the travelers had found it a mite hard to climb out of bed. Yet the moment Copper opened her eyes, she breathed a prayer of gratitude; the Sniders' nightmare had ended as they had all prayed it would. Once again Copper's morning prayer centered on her own healing and relief from pain as soon as possible.

The rain let up enough for the daily school lesson at noon, but it soon intensified again. Copper had grinned when little Carrie had brought her picture book *Mother Goose* and climbed on the teacher's lap as the session ended. Copper barely had time for more than a few hurried pages before Redlin called for the wagons to move out.

"This rain is shore going to affect the river," Adele fretted.

"Maybe by tomorrow it will be over." Copper settled snugly under the blanket. She'd done what she promised herself she wouldn't do. Moments before the wagon train moved on, she'd snuck a dropperful of laudanum, and now the medicine had begun to counteract the persistent inferno in her right foot.

Soon, Lord. Soon. Let this be finished with the best possible outcome. I'll accept whatever you will, but I cannot imagine how I can live in this pain forever.

Did God care about one woman's anguish? Copper believed that he did. Without that belief she couldn't have mustered enough strength to continue this journey.

"Those wagons are still following us," Adele noted.

Copper, too relaxed to talk, murmured, "I told Josh that he should have let me handle it."

"Josh, is it?"

"Redlin, then." She yawned. "The Grand Potentate."

"You should be ashamed of yourself."

She yawned. "I am."

By mid-afternoon the downpour slackened to a faint mist. Redlin gathered the travelers for a short meeting.

"We reach the river tomorrow. Mike tells me it's running pretty hard but crossable. That's the good news. We should have all the wagons across by late afternoon." His gaze sought Copper's. "We'll reach Fort Riceson by mid-afternoon the next day. I'm going to stay behind with Miss Wilson until she's well enough to make the return trip to Thunder Ridge."

"You'll take her back?" Sadie asked.

"Dyson will provide an escort. It's only a few days' ride to Thunder Ridge on horseback."

"What about those snobs behind us?"

"What about the Newsomes?"

"They're still on our tail."

Redlin removed his hat and drew a hand through thick reddish hair streaked by the sun. "I'm well aware they haven't left us."

"What do you intend to do about them?"

"Nothing. They've made their choice. We'll cross the river and move on."

Copper seriously doubted his commitment to the plan. This much she knew about Josh Redlin; he had a heart as big as all outdoors. The only way he'd ignore the needs of those fancy pants was if the good Lord struck him blind.

When they reached that river, there'd be trouble. Copper didn't have a doubt in her mind.

*　*　*

At eight A.M. the wagons rolled out, and by mid-morning Copper could hear the faint sound of rushing water. Anxiety about the unknown began to build inside her.

Directly ahead, the Buffalo was out of its banks and running fast. Swallowing hard, she studied the sight. Scant hours beyond the turbulent barrier lay relief, the end of this constant, grating hurt.

Redlin halted the wagons several hundred feet back from the rising waters. Grass grew rank along the roadside.

Several men climbed from wagon seats and joined Josh and Richardson at water's edge.

This morning Adele's wagon traveled mid-center of the pack. Copper leaned out of the seat to peer back at the dozen or so wagons following. In the distance she spotted the New-somes' party.

Copper whirled, lips firmed. "Those people are planning to cross with us."

Adele shook her head. "Wanting and doing are two different matters. Redlin warned them to stay back."

"Yes, but it's one thing to issue a warning and another to carry it out." If it was up to her, she'd make that pampered Milly Newsome get out of bed and swim across the river with those frivolous dresses strapped to her back.

But then she wasn't as caring as Josh, actually. The thought gave her pause. She was selfish. Willful. She didn't care for the sudden comprehension, but short of shooting the New-somes, Copper didn't see how Josh could stop them. He didn't have to give protection but he couldn't prevent them from following in their wake. Her temper churned.

The intruders' lead wagon gradually drew near. A black man reined up behind the last Redlin wagon and wrapped the lines around the brake. Climbing off the seat, he walked to the water's edge and approached the wagon master, hat in hand.

Copper reached for her crutches. "Come on, Adele. And hurry."

"Oh Lordy me. I knew I shouldn't have got up this morning."

By the time the two women reached the men they were deep into conversation. Josh's deep timbre remained collected. "I told Mr. Newsome that he's on his own."

The Negro man worried his hat in his hands. "Yes sir, I heard it myself, but Mr. Newsome says I'm to tell you that he's ready to join up now."

Join up? Of all the— Copper bit down hard on her tongue. If Redlin agreed, she would personally wring his neck!

Josh shook his head, and then after a moment said, "Tell Mr. Newsome that he's welcome. We'll get him and his family safely across."

The black nodded, then turned and nodded to the women.

Copper's jaw dropped. She confronted Adele. "Did he say what I thought he just said?"

The older woman nodded. "Unless my hearing's going, along with everything else."

The men broke up and Copper hobbled to Redlin, heat creeping up her cheeks. "How could you!"

Settling his hat on his head, Josh kept walking. "Better find something to occupy your time. We got a long day ahead of us."

She trailed along behind him, so angry she was nearly

speechless. "How *could* you let those . . . those people do this when you clearly told them to keep their wagons back."

"I haven't got time to argue with you, Copper. Go find something to occupy your time."

She was in his face now. "You promised, Josh. You promised to take care of this situation. Those wagons will delay us." And the pain in her ankle didn't permit her to accept even the slightest hitch in plans.

He snapped, "Go to your wagon."

"You promised—even God would object to this."

He paused. Then turned and met her eyes. "Your God or my God? My God is a God of peace."

The remark stopped her short. Of all the— Her faith had never been questioned. "As is my God." Her God was just as big as his God, but God had rules. Didn't Redlin have rules? Rules he kept?

"Then go to your wagon. We're about to cross the river, and we'll need your cooperation." He walked away, leaving her to stew in her own juices. And yet guilt filled her, the spiritual kind that stings the conscience. The kind where you know you're wrong and the other person's right and your behavior has just shown you are no better than the person you've condemned.

She didn't like the emotion. She didn't like the feeling or herself in general. And she sure didn't like Redlin for his part in causing the sensation and not keeping his word.

Getting what now had grown to thirty-two rigs—counting the three families the soldiers had added—across the roiling Buffalo was more difficult than she had allowed herself to imagine. As she studied the turbulent current she suddenly realized, with her heart more than just with her head, that lives might be lost in the next few hours. The river was still rising. By evening the river would be up so much that crossing might be impossible. For the first several yards of the passage the water was only knee-deep, but it was anybody's guess how bottomless it was in the middle of the stream.

The men unpacked cross saws and cut down enough thick, sturdy trees growing along the riverbank to build a raft that could hold one wagon and two horses. That was all that could be taken across at one time. If a family had four horses, two were unhitched and made to swim across. The raft was drawn close to the bank and a rig and team were driven on board. Some of the horses refused to step onto it and had to be unhitched and replaced.

Several men worked to pull the raft across the river by ropes attached to the opposite shore. Two men would stand on the front part of the platform and get a firm grip on the rope. Turning their backs to the opposite shore, they would start walking toward the back. As soon as they reached the stern two more men would do the same thing. This arduous relay was repeated until the raft reached the other side.

Copper sat on the bank all day, watching the activity, still seething inside at the Newsomes' waiting rigs.

Once, the black man started to the river to help and Newsome summoned him back with an angry retort. By late afternoon most of party was across, with only Adele's and the Louisiana rigs waiting to cross. Adele told Josh to get the Newsomes' wagons across before she lost her mind. They'd wait to cross last, grateful for the silence.

Granted, it was getting near suppertime and no one had much extra patience, but Milly Newsome was a disgrace.

Shortly after lunch she tired of the slow crossing procedure and began to complain loudly and often.

Around four she demanded that the Negro servants build a fire and cook thick steaks and fire-roasted potatoes, while the Redlin party, hungry, tired, and wet, grunted and hauled wagons across the water. Reginald Newsome stood back with one hand in his watch fob pocket and watched the activity.

Florence Newsome prowled beside their wagon dressed in silks and a large hat with a billowing black feather. Her carping echoed up and down the riverbank.

Milly's strident demands carried across the water. "I am tired of this! When do we cross? Father! Why must we cross last?"

Occasionally Florence would seem to be struck with some adult impulse and make a weak effort to quiet her daughter, but it was to no avail. Reginald seemed not to notice any of it. The long afternoon wore on Copper. At times it was like seeing a mirrored imagine of her and some of the fits she'd been known to pitch, and she didn't like the reminder.

Lord, this is unfair. I know there's a lesson in this, and I know what you're telling me, but this is plain upsetting to watch.

The self-analysis was painful, but try as she might she could not ignore the similarity.

Once the young woman threw herself on the ground (in her satin dress and slippers) and demanded that her father do *something* to hurry the process.

As she watched a whipped man try to control a selfish, rebellious young girl, God's lesson became more and more clear to her. She was witnessing her life until she injured her foot. Hours passed, endless minutes that she became increasingly repentant of the times she had berated Josh. She began to feel that perhaps this was God's way of punishing her as well as educating her.

When it came time to move the Newsome wagons, the blacks doused the cooking fire and readied the wagons.

Amid panicky screams and bellicose demands, the four wagons were ferried across the swollen river with no damage other than the loss of Florence's hat. The chapeau, black feather bobbing, was last seen as it swept around the first bend downriver. Copper's ride was the last to load. Adele drove the rig onto the platform, and the men ferried it across. On the opposite bank, cooking fires gave off wondrous smells of beans and fried pies.

Josh lifted Copper out of the wagon, and gently set her on the ground. Their gazes locked. His windblown wet features evidenced the strain of the day. She had sorely misjudged this man. His patience knew no limit.

"Are you angry with me?" he asked softly.

"I'm very proud of you."

Reprieve broke across his rugged features. "It didn't slow us down much. We couldn't have traveled until dawn, and as you can see, the Newsomes aren't capable of traveling alone."

That was the understatement of the year.

She'd hardly realized that her arms remained around his neck. Surroundings faded as she gazed deeply into his eyes for the first time. Who was this man and what—or who—had brought him to this hour, this moment with her? A day ago she could have listed fifty faults, but at this moment only his strong points came to mind. Most men would have held to their word and made the Newsome wagons cross alone. After such a clear warning, most men would have gone on and never looked back. But not this man. He had extended the same courtesy and protection to Reginald and Florence Newsome that he gave the whole train.

They stood, gazing into each other's eyes until Adele walked by and broke it up.

"Hey you two. Supper's waiting, and you're creating a spectacle."

Smiling, Copper grappled for the crutch. "Oh hush up, Adele, at least it's a good spectacle."

And that, she thought, *is better than the trouble I've been making.*

Adele chuckled. "I stand corrected. At least you two weren't going at it like a couple of drunken cowhands on payday."

"Well." Copper grinned up at Josh. "The day isn't over yet."

Chapter 14

Sadie had decided to ride with a family who had a fussy infant this morning. The young mother needed to drive while the husband helped with the stock.

Redlin's horse pulled even with Adele's wagon and he touched the brim of his hat. "Morning, ladies."

"And a cold one it is," Adele grumbled. "My old bones tell me I'm not getting any younger."

Copper couldn't resist throwing a tease to the handsome wagon master. "How is Miss Newsome this morning?" The young woman had started shamelessly hanging around the man, demanding attention. Over breakfast this morning Copper had been tempted to douse her with a bucket of cold water to cool her ardor.

"I believe Mrs. Newsome is feeling fine," he replied.

Copper fixed her eyes on the road. "I meant Milly."

"Oh. Milly."

"Yes. Oh Milly." If he didn't watch himself he'd be hogtied

by the time the train reached its destination. Milly Newsome was not accustomed to being denied whatever she wanted. And in this case it was becoming more and more obvious she had her eye on the wagon master.

He turned pensive but she could easily see through his repartee. "Quite a woman. Real spirited. The way I like my women."

"Yes. Quite." Copper crossed her arms and vowed to remain civil. She was a new woman; never again would she behave like the old Copper. At least Milly had served her purpose, being the worst example of womanhood ever noted. The old Copper had learned her lesson. All the times she'd argued with him, demanded her way. Fought him at every turn like a spoiled child, called him names behind his back—like a child. Those days were over. She'd seen what an ugly creature she'd become, and with God's help she would change her wayward ways.

"Yes," he mused, settling the brim of his hat lower against the chilly drizzle. "Quite a woman."

Copper realized that he saw right through her and relished her misery and plain old jealously toward Milly, whom he couldn't possibly give a whit about.

"Sweet kid," he noted. "Shame she'll be nothing but a burden to society." He nudged the horse's side and rode ahead.

Adele threw back her head and hooted. "That man. He purely loves to devil you."

Mid-morning Richardson rode by and paused to visit. The mist thickened and the clouds ahead seemed to be eating up the horizon. "Morning, ladies."

They greeted the assistant wagon master in unison.

He peered up, eyes assessing the overcast ceiling. "I'll eat my hat if it doesn't snow."

"Snow!" Copper sat up straighter. "A real snow—this early?"

He shrugged. "Not all that early. I lived in these parts when I was a young'un. I've seen many a snow this time of year, but it won't stay on the ground long."

Copper settled back. By evening they would be enjoying a warm meal and soft bed at Fort Riceson so the weather didn't matter.

Richardson glanced at her foot propped on a storage box. "Won't be long now."

She smiled. "Can't be soon enough for me. When do you reckon we'll get there?" Though the weather was nasty it hadn't slowed the morning's progress.

"Should be there by early afternoon. I think Josh wants to push on through and skip the noon stop. That's what I'm here to tell you. Sadie sent word that she's fixing a couple of biscuits and ham for you two. I'll drop them by closer to noon." He kneed the stallion and rode on.

"That's mighty kind," Adele remarked.

"Sadie's a good heart. It's a shame some man hasn't noticed her qualities."

The older woman turned to look at her. "I wasn't talking about Sadie. I was referring to Josh. Open your eyes, woman. The man's in love with you and he's worried sick about that ankle."

The observation caught Copper off guard. She knew that her and Josh's former animosity was almost forced now, but for Adele to suggest that the wagon master was in love with her? That was too much to hope for. "Don't be silly. We've simply called a truce. The weather's getting bad and he's eager to reach the fort so I can see the doctor, and the folks can have a day or two to rest and warm up before you go on to Colorado Springs."

Josh. In love with her. She couldn't deny that the thought was appealing.

"A truce, huh? That's what all that eye gazing was about last night?"

Copper shrugged, pulling her cloak tighter. "It was getting dark; it was hard to see."

Adele whistled to the team and avoided a pothole. "I can die peacefully. I've heard it all now."

Minutes stretched before Copper ventured, "Even if he were to . . . have affection for me, what about this Susan person?" Lately the name had hung in the back of her mind. Who was this woman and why did Josh correspond with her? She thought she knew Redlin well enough now to know she wasn't a wife or even a love interest. Everything she had observed about the man had indicated the highest moral standards. He spoke to women respectfully, and while vile language poured from some of the men's mouths, Copper had never heard Josh utter a single profanity. Goodness knew he'd had plenty of opportunities to let curses fly, yet he always spoke politely and cleanly. If women were within earshot, he insisted the other men limit their profanity. But the idea that this man, this man for whom her respect had grown by leaps and bounds in the past few days, could actually be in love with her stole her breath.

God, if that is true I am certainly unworthy of his love. He deserves more than a hotheaded, temperamental, selfish redhead like me. Then, from some deep deposit of feminine competition, she added, *But so is a spoiled blond like Milly unworthy of him.*

Shortly before noon, Richardson galloped up with the sack of biscuits and ham. The wagon train paused for a brief rest stop and a change of drivers.

Within minutes they were back on the trail, with Sadie now at the reins.

She glanced over and grinned at Copper. "Not going to be long now. Richardson said the fort's about an hour away."

Copper bit into a cold biscuit and closed her eyes in ecstasy with the thought of a soft bed, hot coffee, warm meals, and Dr. Dale Dyson. Soon now she would know if the injury could be treated. Could the doctor work a miracle and do what the average doctor couldn't? Would his gift of healing and medical training allow her to walk freely and easily again?

"I pray Dyson will be able to help," she said softly, finding courage a little harder to muster when the end of the trip was so near.

"That's all our prayers, but you're a strong woman and you'll live with whatever comes your way." Sadie shook her head. "When I lost my husband I swore I couldn't go on—I couldn't find a purpose to live anymore. But every morning I'd open my eyes to a new day. Sometimes I'd be angry with God and demand to know why he took my man and left me. Didn't seem right to throw a woman out in this world alone. Then one morning I opened my eyes and that black veil that'd hung over my head for almost a year didn't feel as heavy. Every day afterward the load got a little easier, and now I'm on my way to make a new life. I still miss my man, miss him a lot, but I know he's in a far better place and I ain't got the heart to wish him back. Love's like that, you know."

Copper didn't know. Until she'd met Josh she'd not given that kind of selfless, lifelong love much thought. She always figured when it came, it came. Otherwise, she'd content herself with teaching and living an independent life. Somehow and somewhere between here and Beeder's Cove her values had changed. Right now the love of a good man sounded mighty good. A man she could trust, respect, and, yes, lean on. She desperately needed a pair of strong male arms around her, assuring her that all would be well even though she didn't always believe it. She was beginning to realize that she could not expect life to be perfect. She was starting to suspect the trick to a happy life here on earth was acceptance. Acquire the ability to face life head-on, and when circumstances ambush you, you get up and limp to the finish line with whatever the good Lord has left you.

She reached up to swipe at hot tears suddenly rolling down her cheeks and noticed the fine mist was turning to rain/snow. "Look, Sadie. It's snowing."

"Why it shore is. Will you look at that?" Fat, lazy flakes the size of peas soon filled the air. A whoop went up and down the line, and children's excited laughter filled the air. Was any sight as uplifting as the first snowfall of the season or as heartening as the last one?

Copper reached out to catch the flakes on her hand. The snow melted as quickly as it touched the ground. The sight was so pretty she took it as a harbinger of things to come. For the first time since she'd begun the arduous journey, she felt capable of facing whatever obstacles lay ahead of her.

Mid-afternoon Fort Riceson came into view. Amid swirling snow, the whoops and cheers echoed up and down the line.

Sadie looked over and grinned. "Everyone on this train loves you, honey. We've all been praying for this moment."

Tears rolled down Copper's cheeks. She'd be leaving this wonderful family soon. The thought hit her almost like a physical blow. She would miss every one of them so very much.

The catcalls and happy cheers continued as Josh rode up, grinning. "You're here, Miss Wilson. And only a few days late."

She smiled. "I forgive you, Mr. Redlin. You said you'd get me here safe and sound, and you're a man of your word."

His features sobered. "That I am." Their gazes held momentarily before he announced. "I'll ride ahead and let them know who we are." He scanned the distant fort and frowned. "Surprised there's not a welcoming committee."

Copper's gaze skimmed the area. The fort was remote, but she'd heard there was a large contingent here.

Sadie turned to look. "Does seem a might peculiar. They are expecting us, aren't they?"

Josh nodded. "They know we're coming." He kneed the horse and moved ahead. Richardson fell in beside him, and the two men rode toward the fortress.

Copper glanced at Sadie and grinned. "I'm glad the trip is over, but I'm going to miss you and Adele."

"It's over for you," she said. "We still got a lot of road before us. I'm looking forward to a couple of days' rest before we move on."

The wagons sat waiting word from Redlin and Richardson. Word came down the line that Milly Newsome demanded to know why the delay?

Without disguising the disgust in her voice, Copper began, "If that woman was here I'd tell her to—"

"—have a nice day," said Sadie with a smile.

Crossing her arms, Copper turned back to face the fort. "I don't envy you spending more days on the trail with that one."

"That bunch don't bother me. Someone said they'll be leaving us once we cross the last river."

Snow flew, sweeping the rugged landscape like a giant broom. Copper would be so happy to be warm again, to climb between sweet-smelling sheets and sleep without interruption. Adele was a saint, but a snoring saint. Many a night Copper plugged her ears with cotton, but she couldn't block out the wheezing snorts.

Minutes ticked past. Ten turned to twenty.

Teeth chattering, Copper muttered. "What is taking them so long?"

Sadie's mood had gone from elated to pensive. "Don't know—it don't seem right." Her eyes scanned the distant fort. "Don't look to be a thing stirring."

Biting her lower lip, Copper fixed on the scene before her. Any minute now Josh and Frank would ride out and give the signal to move forward.

Any minute.

Chapter 15

$\operatorname{\boldsymbol{\boldsymbol{-}}}$

"I can't wait any longer." Copper reached for the crutch. "I'm going up there."

Sadie laid a restraining hand on her arm. "Don't do it." The solemnity in her words stopped Copper from following her instinct.

"Sadie, something must be wrong or they would be back by now. How long does it take to announce our arrival?"

"Can't say, but we wait until Redlin or Richardson signals us."

More minutes ticked by, anxious minutes. Sadie kept a firm hold on Copper's arm.

Finally, Richardson rode through the fort gate. As he drew closer, Copper distinguished his grave demeanor. Hope plummeted.

"Dr. Dyson must be gone," Copper said in little more than a whisper.

"Now, now, you don't know that," Sadie cautioned. "Don't

be borrowing trouble. By the look on Richardson's face, we may already have enough."

Richardson rode straight to their wagon. Reining up, he nodded. "Miss Copper. Mrs. Fortright."

Amid her chaotic thoughts Sadie's married name registered. Copper didn't think she'd ever heard it mentioned. She swallowed. "The doctor's gone, isn't he?"

"Ma'am, if you would, Josh wants me to bring you to the fort."

Sadie started to drive the wagon forward, but Richardson stopped her. "Just Miss Wilson. Mrs. Fortright, Josh wants you to hold the wagons here. Circle them tight for the night."

The woman nodded. "Shore will. What's wrong?"

He touched the brim of his hat. "Circle 'em tight, Mrs. Fortright. And tell Mike to put on extra guards."

Richardson reached over and helped Copper move off the wagon seat and straddle his horse behind the saddle. He was well into his fifties, but he still had the arm strength of a man much younger. He urged the stallion into a gallop. Copper held tightly to the assistant wagon master's waist. Her ankle throbbed with each jolt, but the pain barely registered due to the multitude of questions that raced through her mind.

As the animal slowed and walked through the fort's open double gates, she suddenly felt bile rise to the back of her throat. Practically nothing was standing, except for a portion of a building along the front wall. The barracks, the mess hall, even the hitching posts were only burned relics. Richardson removed his bandana and reached back to hand it to her. She clamped the cloth over her nose, despair engulfing her. Bodies were everywhere.

"Kiowa massacre. Look at the shields. They're made of buffalo hides, and the weapons are bows and lances. His eyes scanned the scores of bodies wearing buckskin, with paint and feathers. There were more than a hundred soldiers and some civilians here. Not sure how many women and children. Can't know if any patrols were out at the time. We can only pray that they were." His eyes scanned the destruction. "Maybe we ought to thank the good Lord that none survived. It would take all a man possessed to come back to this."

She stifled the instinct to rail at God for allowing this injustice, but only gratitude filled her heart. But for the small interruptions, the wagon train would have been here and met the same fate.

Yet her destiny was sealed. With Dyson's death—and the scene seemed to assure that such was true—she was certain to be crippled for life.

Richardson nudged his mount across the compound. Some of the charred rubble still gave off small plumes of smoke. They approached the blackened wall of the sole remaining building, where Redlin's horse stood. The fort's back wall was burned to the ground. Apparently the savages rode south thinking the whole structure would burn, but the front of the fort remained intact. Before she could stop it, her imagination started picturing the slaughter that had taken place.

With a sob she choked, "I've seen enough." She buried her face in the back of Richardson's shirt and pleaded, "Please take me back to the wagon."

"Bear with me, Miss Wilson." He reined up and dismounted, and then lifted Copper down off the horse.

"Please, Mr. Richardson, I can't bear any more of this."

Josh met her in the doorway. "Copper. Come in here."

Hesitantly she reached for his outstretched hand and grasped it. Supporting her weight, he led her into the shell of the building that now consisted of only two rooms and a partial roof. She caught sight of a small room on the left. Snow blew through the broken windowpane and dusted the dirt floor. One lone man sat crumpled in a corner, wrapped in a blanket and staring at a near-empty gin bottle. It took a moment for her to realize what she was looking at.

"Who is it?" she asked.

"If this envelope that was in his pocket belongs to him, it's Dr. Dyson."

Josh pulled her close to his side. "I found him like this. I haven't been able to get a word out of him." His eyes wandered to a far corner where an Indian woman lay, gravely wounded. She wore a beaded buckskin tunic and skirt, now coated in dried blood. Her long hair was braided and filthy. She tossed on a pallet, murmuring indistinguishable phrases.

Breaking away from Josh, Copper went to kneel awkwardly in front of Dyson, a man with a vacant face covered by grime and beard. She reached for his hand and found that it was icy to the touch. "Doctor?"

Rheumy brown eyes fixed on the bottle.

Copper tried to rub warmth in his cold fingers. "We need blankets."

Richardson turned. "I'll bring some from the wagons."

"And hot coffee," Copper called. "All you can carry."

Josh took the man's shoulders and straightened him out on the floor. Copper took the lone blanket in the room and wrapped it snugly around the doctor.

"I'll start a fire." Josh moved to break up a few random pieces of furniture that had been spared by the flames.

Richardson returned with blankets and hot soup and coffee. Copper spent the afternoon spooning drops of hot liquid into the doctor's mouth and doing what she could for the injured woman. Her injuries were so grave Copper couldn't believe she was still alive. She refused all substances that Copper offered.

At first Dyson resisted her efforts, but eventually he calmed and obediently swallowed when the metal spoon touched his dried lips.

Late afternoon Josh said, "We need to get him out of here and into a wagon."

Copper nudged broth between the doctor's lips. "Who has the space?" Every wagon was filled to near capacity with family or personal possessions, and it was unlikely the Newsomes would voluntarily unload any of their excesses.

"Some family will have to unload for the time being." Josh nodded toward the doctor. "He won't make it much longer in these kinds of temperatures."

Copper's eyes turned to the woman. "And her?"

"She won't make it through the night. Regardless."

Richardson spoke up. "The Addison family, a young man and his new bride. Joined up at the last checkpoint. They'll help out."

By suppertime, the doctor was relocated to the wagon. After much discussion, it was decided they would leave the woman where she was and someone would sit with her until the end came.

Dyson remained in a near-catatonic state, eyes fixed and staring. But by bedtime Copper detected a change. His limbs twitched and he tossed on the pallet, muttering indecipherably.

"I don't know what he needs," Copper told Josh. The two sat beside the doctor while Jack and Marie Addison slept in Adele's wagon.

"Gin," Josh said. "The liquor's wearing off and he needs a drink."

"We don't have gin." She glanced up. "Do we?"

"I expect I could confiscate a bottle among the men, but I don't think it's in the doctor's best interest."

"What do we do?"

"Well." Josh took off his hat and rubbed his temple. "I'd say we brace ourselves for a rough ride. He'll be drying out, and it's not a pretty sight."

Redlin again proved his knack for understatement.

The following two days turned hellish. The Indian woman refused to die. She was so near death you could smell the stench, and yet her chest rose and fell with each breath. Copper tried to stay put in Adele's wagon but she couldn't. She wanted to help, and she babied the ankle, but she couldn't sit and do nothing. This morning she had Richardson take her to the fort. There was so little to do other than make the dying woman as comfortable as possible, and pray for mercy. The woman remained in a deep sleep or thrashed about, unable or unwilling to take nourishment.

Adele and Sadie stayed with the doctor throughout his "drying out" period. Screams of imagined terror filled the night air as the man thrashed about on his pallet, claiming poisonous spiders were climbing on the canvas walls. Explosive outbursts and vile cursing echoed through the camp when Adele and Sadie failed to kill the imaginary bugs.

Copper sat and prayed in Adele's rocker that had thoughtfully been moved to the Addisons' wagon. There was little more she could do, and Josh wouldn't permit her to be on the ankle for more than a few minutes at a time. After a particularly harrowing episode when the doctor threatened to take a gun and kill them all, Copper had lashed out at Josh because he wouldn't let her out of the wagon.

"Why does it matter," she'd yelled after three long days of waiting. "I'll always be a cripple! Whatever is wrong will never be right because it has been too long. The bones are starting to knit and there's nothing we can do now!" The only man on earth who could offer hope was thrashing around on a pallet, out of his mind.

Later she would look back on that time and marvel at Redlin's tenacity, and how easily she had slipped back into her old ways. Milly was forgotten; the old Copper had surfaced and she was ashamed. Josh had absorbed all the anger and despair she threw at him, and then rationally, and with resolve, restated his order. He had more trouble than he could handle, while her temporary state of compliance and humility had faded in the face of despair and fear. And still he remained calm and in control.

The snow squalls soon ended and a weak sun melted what little remained on the ground. All the wagons stayed in the protective circle as the temperatures warmed. All, that was, except the four from Louisiana. On the third morning they pulled out without a by-your-leave to anyone. Not a single soul mentioned their departure. It would seem that not a single soul cared.

The following morning, Copper opened her eyes to si-

lence. She sat up straighter in the rocker, looking for Adele
and Sadie. They weren't in the wagon. Dr. Dyson slept on
the pallet, and for the first time in days he seemed in a rest-
ful slumber, not tossing and turning or ranting wildly.

Adele parted the back canvas. When she spotted Copper
awake, she smiled and whispered, "I'll get your coffee."

Within minutes she returned bearing a steaming mug.
"Here you go."

Copper appreciatively accepted the warmth and inclined
her head toward the patient. "He's better."

Nodding, Adele climbed in the wagon and checked his
pulse. "Sometime during the night he started to calm. He's
sleeping normal now."

"Praise God."

"He's the one that should be praising God. He is lucky to
be alive."

The awful scene she'd witnessed that first day flooded
Copper's mind. "Oh Adele, it was appalling. Nothing inside
the fort escaped, and the stench was unbelievable. Men,
women, animals. Kiowa. All had met a brutal death."

Adele straightened. "Don't let yourself think about it,
honey. If you do you'll lose your mind. Man's inhumanity to
one another is hard to swallow."

Copper wanted the images wiped from her mind. She
could only imagine the horrors the doctor had witnessed.
How did he manage to escape the onslaught when nothing
else was spared? He must have been outside the grounds
that day—or night. Empathy burned deep in her soul.
Had he ridden home to find the fort, and all those within,
destroyed? Had he lost his wife . . . and maybe some children? Her gaze fixed on the man on the pallet, and she

wondered if they were doing him any favor by fighting for his life.

Even worse, would the good doctor consider their efforts humanitarian or appallingly inhumane?

"Miss Wilson?"

Copper glanced up later that evening to see one of her noon students standing before her. The boy's hat was in his hand.

"Yes, Jake?"

He inclined his head to the fort. "This is a time we ought to fear? Right?"

"Yes." She drew the boy to her side. "I regret that I chose fear for that particular lesson, Jake. I'd noticed how frightened the children were when we passed Indians along the road, and I had wanted to point out that all Indians aren't savages. Some are peaceful, but yes, there are those who are evil, same as white men. Some are very wicked and cause things like this to happen. But I have no explanation as to why it happens."

How did you convince a ten-year-old to practice selective fear? Was that in the realm of possibility for anyone?

The boy turned to stare at the fort. He had no idea what lay behind those gates, and she prayed to God that he would never witness such carnage and savagery. Yet death's stench permeated the air and he had heard talk. As much as the adults wanted to shield their young from man's brutality, it was impossible.

He turned back, grave-faced. "If God loves everybody, why does he let something like this happen?"

Powerless to explain, she mutely shook her head. Her fancy

schooling might have equipped her to educate young minds, but all of Papa's wealth couldn't have purchased a sensible answer for Jake, or for her. Yet, deep down, she knew there had to be one. The ultimate cruelty would be for things like this to happen and there not be an answer.

It was those *becauses* and *whys* in her life that she struggled to understand and accept.

Chapter 16

The nightly fire burned low. Overhead, a quarter moon rose in the west. Families had retired hours ago, but sleep eluded Copper. Her mind refused to release the long day. All hope was dashed. Dr. Dyson lay in the Addison wagon either sleeping or staring sightlessly at the canvas ceiling. Funny thing, hope. Hers had temporarily spiked earlier in the day when the doctor appeared to rally, but he still had not responded to anyone. Not when she'd tried to spoon broth between his lips, not when she'd tried to rouse him. The obvious started to emerge; whatever world Dale Dyson had joined, he had no intentions of returning to this one. Not of his own choice.

"It's late. You should be asleep."

Copper scooted over to allow Redlin to share her seat on the log that Mike had dragged up to the wagon to serve as a bench for Copper. Logic told her they should move away from the wagon and not disturb Adele, but she felt there was little chance of waking either her friend or Dr. Dyson.

Josh settled on the feed sack that was supposed to serve to keep britches and skirts dry. He removed his hat. "Not a time I'd care to relive."

Copper nodded in silent agreement. Not a person on earth should face this carnage.

"The woman?"

"Still breathing."

He reached for her hand. For a long moment he studied the appendage. She wondered if she'd suddenly sprouted warts, but then it became apparent that he was just plain talked out. He'd conjectured, cried, consoled, and prayed with so many today, he didn't have anything left to give.

Her hand slipped from his, and gently she made him more comfortable. He settled against the wagon bed like a man who was bone weary of responsibility.

Silence fell like a cozy blanket. Only an occasional log dropping deeper into the fire broke the stillness.

Her arm drifted around his shoulder, and her fingers through his hair, and she lightly massaged his scalp, easing tension. She, Audrey, and Willow had used the calming technique on one another so many times she didn't think about propriety. If it weren't for her, he'd be farther down the road, closer to Colorado Springs, closer to whatever waited in his future. Longing for Dallas? She watched the moon rise, softly working her fingers through the thick reddish mass. She couldn't count the troubles she'd brought this man's way, yet it was he who spoke her thoughts.

"I'm sorry."

Shaking her head, she smiled. "I thought you'd fallen asleep."

"No, I won't sleep tonight. Got too many thoughts running through my head."

"Such as?"

"If we'd gotten here a day or two earlier—"

"But we didn't." She gently tapped his scalp in rebuke. "Besides, who knows when this awful thing happened?"

"Three, four days at the most."

"Then the delays were a blessing." She hadn't thought so at the time, but recently more than one event had reminded her that often her time schedule was not as good as God's.

The solemnity of her reflection struck home and she thought of Willow. Willow would say that nothing happened by accident; the hand of God had spared their lives for whatever purpose.

Josh groaned. "I'm so tired of misery."

She thumped his head soundly.

"Okay—but I am. Tired of life."

"Oh Josh." She gently lifted his head upright and forced him to meet her eyes. "You can't lose heart. You're the one who keeps us going, the one we look to for guidance."

He refused the role. "I have no right to lead anyone."

Today had proved to be too much. Living with devastation day after day; he'd reached his limit. This man read his Bible nightly and accepted people like the Newsomes without judgment, so when he lost heart, what hope did others have? "Don't talk that way. You scare me."

"I should scare you."

She massaged the knotted ligaments in his neck. "If not

you, then who?" There were many able-bodied men in the train, but none as responsible as he. Richardson came to mind, and she weighed the men's strengths and weaknesses, and Josh still won out.

"It will get better," she said, because she knew the healing of her injury lay heavy on his heart. The delays, which now proved to be a good thing, had been a weight around his neck. "I have one good foot, and I can always teach. Naturally I've prayed for the best, but apparently God has his reasons for denying me. Willow contends that he doesn't close one door without opening a window, and I'm going to trust that the window he opens is better than any I could ever imagine."

He sighed, sitting up. "What happened to the Copper Wilson I met in Thunder Ridge?"

"Oh, she's still around—more often than I care for her to be. But I've grown some." She shifted. "You know, there's this really strange family in Thunder Ridge, and I rather hope to teach their children someday. The Parneckers, and they have nine children, all named Ralph."

"Nine boys?"

"No. Nine girls and boys. Named them all Ralph so when the parents call they all come running. I don't know if that's brilliant or just plain lazy. Anyway, Willow would have had the children this semester but then she got kicked in the head by that horse and—well, you know the story."

"No one thought she'd live, but she did and she married Tucker Gray a few Saturdays back. Audrey agreed to assume the Thunder Ridge teaching position since Willow can't until she regains her strength. Audrey's teaching job in Blackberry Hill fell through, and work is slow at the Burying Parlor."

She grinned. "You do pay attention."

"I have to. I have a feeling you don't."

"Wrong. Admittedly I'm a little stubborn and I learn my lessons the hard way. It's taken a rough road to make me see the real Copper." She chuckled. "I know God sent Milly Newsome to open my eyes to my flawed nature."

"On your nastiest day, you were never as bad as Milly. And I can say that because I'm fairly certain that I've witnessed some of your worst days."

Well, it was a backhanded compliment, but she'd take it. "Thank you, I think. Now that you know who I am, who are you?"

He leaned back and rested his head against the wagon bed. "Just a man. A very tired man."

"You're more than a man. You have a past."

"Do I?"

"Don't you?"

"Not one I'd care to discuss, if that's what you're getting at."

"Then a future? What's your dream, Josh Redlin? Land? Power? Money?"

"Dry socks."

"That's not a dream. We all want that."

"Peace on earth."

The man was able to avoid what he didn't want to discuss. She tried a different tack. "Are your folks alive?"

"I think my pa is. Last I heard, he was in California. Haven't seen the man since I was ten years old. Ma took us kids and went east with her folks because she had health problems, and Pa chose to stay behind."

"Sorry."

"Feel sorry for him. He has four sons who don't know him."

"Then you have siblings."

"Three brothers. You?"

"Only child. My folks died on an ocean voyage a few years back. I was teaching in Texas by then and remained behind. My biggest regret is that they never realized how much I loved my work, and them. They thought I had turned away from family, but all I wanted was to fulfill my dream to teach. Papa was quite wealthy by inheritance, but by the time the Yankees came and burned Timber Creek, most of it was gone. They took or destroyed whatever was left."

"How did you survive?"

"There were only ten or so of us that remained in Timber Creek through the war—Willow, Audrey, Asa Jeeters—the town drunk—and five women from the congregation. We were storing canned goods in the church cellar when the Yanks rode through. When we heard the commotion we hid."

"They didn't check cellars?"

"They checked, but some of us climbed onto the upper shelves and flattened ourselves behind jars of fruit and vegetables. The others hid in a small dug out area covered by a curtain along the back wall. A corporal took a quick look and slammed the cellar door shut."

"And then you and your friends took up arms."

She smiled. "You listen closely."

He grinned. "I know all about your life. I've heard it repeated enough in Thunder Ridge." He reached out and tugged a lock of her hair. "I'd like to see you face off with a Yank."

"I was formidable."

"I can imagine."

"Ah . . . Thunder Ridge." Her tone turned dreamy. "I used to resent that town and all its rain. I didn't know how good I had it."

"We seldom do until something worse comes along." His manner indicated that he'd seen his share of extremes.

Copper sighed. "Sometimes I wish so fervently to be back there. I wonder how things are going between Audrey and Eli. He loved his Genevieve so dearly."

"A man can love two women, but in a different way. Audrey's patience will win out. The man's in love with her."

She glanced his way. Was he thinking of Susan now? "You don't know Eli that well, do you?"

"I don't have to know him to see how he looks at her. You forget that I spent a few weeks watching the relationship grow. He's in love, but he's fighting it."

She smiled. "Why would a man fight the inevitable?"

"Because the man doesn't yet know what is inevitable and what isn't."

This particular man was such a contradiction. Full of empathy one moment, fatalistic the next. She returned to the prior topic. "So . . . you have three brothers, and an estranged father in California."

"If that's what I said."

"You did. You just said so."

"Then it has to be true."

But he'd not mentioned one word about Susan in Dallas. "No sisters?"

"Nary a one."

Before she realized it, the word slipped out. "Wife?"

He paused. "Wife?"

"Yes. Wife. I noticed that you write often to a Susan in Dallas." There. She'd said it and she'd give anything to take the inquiry back, but it was too late.

His features closed and he sat upright. "Anyone ever tell you that you talk too much?"

"No one but you, and I rarely listen to what you have to say."

"If I had a wife, I wouldn't be sitting here with you."

Sobering, she realized that she had overstepped her bounds and she had to salvage what she could of the brief but personal conversation. "You mentioned that you thought the fort attack was fairly recent?"

He nodded wordlessly.

"Then the savages are still in the area?"

"Most likely."

"What about the Newsomes? They took off yesterday morning, alone."

"I sent Richardson after them. He tried to talk sense into Reginald—"

"—of Shreveport," she reminded, since the label seemed to hold such importance with the affluent family.

"Frank warned him they could likely meet the same fate, but he insisted they would travel to the next town and stop. Milly and Florence found the stench here intolerable."

Copper closed her eyes. "They say the Lord takes care of fools and idiots."

"The Newsomes best pray that whoever claims that knows what they're talking about."

Copper didn't want to think about the family meeting the same fate as the soldiers, but the victory at the fort had surely strengthened the Kiowas' bloodlust. Four wagons would not stand a chance. And, of course, the Comanches might find them first.

The moon crept higher. She was glad that all were asleep. Some would find their late night conversation improper, but she sensed that this man needed impropriety tonight. But he wasn't married. The thought rang in her head. Duty rested heavily on his shoulders, and once he took her back to Thunder Ridge, he still had a wagon train to get safely to their destination. Long miles of bad roads, Indians, and threatening weather lay in his future.

Sitting up, he suddenly drew her to him and kissed her. A long, possessive kiss that stole her breath. Too soon for her, their lips parted and their gazes met in the dim light. She wanted to ask why he had chosen that moment for their first kiss, but she'd already made one mistake by inquiring about Susan. She didn't intend to ruin the moment.

She shook her head. "It's late. I should be going inside."

He nodded. "You should." He stood and handed her the crutch.

She knew there was more to be said but she didn't know what. Her feelings at the moment were foreign to anything she'd ever experienced. Was this emotion—this light-headed wooziness—the "love" that Willow spoke of when she talked about Tucker? The feeling was powerful, like being sucked beneath a swift current.

The thought struck her so clearly it might as well have been spoken. She'd gone and fallen in love with this man when she knew nothing about him. Nothing. She parted the back canvas and he gently lifted her into the wagon.

"Good night," she whispered.

"Sleep tight." He leaned over for one more kiss, then

turned and walked off. Her heart was beating so loudly she thought she would wake the whole wagon.

Adele's snores rose from her pallet as Copper put on her nightclothes and crawled between the blankets.

As the moon climbed higher, she stared up at the canvas roof with the very heady taste of Josh Redlin still lingering on her lips.

Chapter 17

A man or woman should have a proper burial. That was the central agreement over breakfast.

"Not much left," one observed. "That Injun, what do we do about her carcass?"

"She's still alive," Josh said. "And the term you're looking for is *body*, Rex. She's a person, not a carcass."

"I'll not dig a hole for the heathen."

"When it's proper, I'll dig her grave." Josh met Copper's eyes. "Ladies, we'll be pulling out tomorrow morning. Ready the wagons."

Copper caught the wagon master as the men manned shovels and picks and headed for the fort. "What about me?"

"Mike's taking you back to Thunder Ridge."

She paused. Back to Thunder Ridge. Once those words would have brought euphoria; now they merely stung.

"Just like that?"

He nodded, muscle working tightly in his left jaw. "Just like that."

"You're not going to take me?" She knew he had little choice in the matter. She couldn't continue on the wagon train with no purpose, even if she weren't a cripple. She'd be a burden to Adele and Sadie during the hundreds of miles of rough land ahead before they reached Colorado Springs. She couldn't push or shove a wagon out of mud. She could barely manage her meals. Nobody wanted or needed extra baggage for the coming weeks, and that's what she'd become. Surplus baggage.

Whirling, she started back to the wagon, willing back tears. What did she expect from Redlin? Did she expect that because he had lowered his guard for the briefest of moments last night, today he'd be a different man? He'd been bone-tired last night. He might not even recall those tender moments she'd taken to heart.

"Copper."

His stern tone made her pause, but she refused to look at him. She couldn't. What if she broke into tears and proved what a hopeless ninny she was? "What?"

"Give me my other choice."

Closing her eyes, reality sank home. He didn't have a choice. His loyalty lay with the wagon train and getting these fine folk to Colorado. He owed her no special treatment other than her being a member of his train—a forced member.

Nodding, she limped on. "I'll be ready by morning." She supposed he nodded; she didn't look. She couldn't.

As she approached the wagon, Sadie stepped out. "There you are. Have you seen Redlin?"

"He's on his way to the fort."

"He needs to see this." She brushed past Copper and hurried off in a trot. Copper's heart sank. Now what? Dyson—

Parting the canvas, Copper spotted Adele bent over the doctor's pallet. She turned when Copper eased into the wagon in a sitting position. "Come look."

Copper turned away. "If he's passed, Adele, have Mike take him to the fort so he can be buried with his company."

A man's deep voice answered. "I haven't passed."

Startled, Copper slowly pulled herself into the wagon and slid to the pallet. Dyson stared up at her, his eyes wet with tears.

"Dr. Dyson?"

He closed his eyes, evidently shutting her out.

She glanced at Adele. "He's responsive?"

Adele nodded. "That's the first words that he's uttered, but he's awake." The older woman bent closer to the patient. "Doctor? Will you try to eat a bite?"

He turned his head.

Copper adjusted the blanket, her eyes pinned to the man. "He can't talk, Adele. It's too soon." Images of the massacre tore at her heart. Surely such memories were consuming this man to the point where he would resent consciousness.

Sadie returned with Josh within the hour. He entered the wagon and knelt beside Dyson and snapped, "Doctor!"

Copper, shocked by his tone, brought a hand to her mouth.

Dyson opened his eyes.

"The name's Redlin. Josh Redlin. We sent word ahead that we would be bringing a young woman to see you."

Josh still spoke in a tone she'd seldom if ever heard. Harsh. Demanding. Couldn't he see this poor man was at the end of his rope?

Dyson covered his head and rolled to his side, but Josh rolled him to his back.

The man struck out, trying to knock his tormentor aside, but Redlin pinned him.

Appalled, Copper cried out, "Leave him alone! Can't you see he's devastated?"

"Stand back, Copper. Now!" Steel tinged his voice.

She stood back. Adele reached gently to move her closer to the back flap. "Honey, I know it seems what he's doing is cruel, but Josh is doing the right thing. Now just hush, and let Redlin handle this."

The doctor met Redlin's eyes. "I need a drink."

"A young woman needs your gift."

Copper watched a silent message play between the two men. One Dyson didn't want, one the wagon master commanded.

Shaking his head, Dyson spoke. "I can't help her."

"If you refuse to help, then you tell her." He reached for Copper and eased her to his side. She met the doctor's gin-soaked eyes, her heart heavy with the request. Hadn't the man been through enough? What right did she have to make impossible demands of him?

"Tell him, Copper," Josh demanded, still in that stringent tone.

"Tell him what?"

"Tell him you've traveled forty miles to seek his help. Days of constant pain, and he's the only hope you have of walking normally. Ask him if gin is more important than the oath that he took to help the sick and injured whenever and wherever he can."

"That's cruel . . ."

"Ask him!"

"Dr. Dyson," she whispered.

He closed his eyes; he was blocking her out. "Please. We see the evidence of what's happened and we can only presume your misery." She reached for his hand. "I know you have seen horrors that I cannot even imagine, but if you would only look at my ankle, just one look, then I can accept my fate and pray that in time you will accept yours. I can't do anything to change what's happened to either one of us. I deeply wish I could. But if you turn me away I'll never know if perhaps you could have altered my life."

"I have no powers," he murmured. "Let me die."

"My understanding is that the good Lord has given you a healing talent few people have."

He slashed back at her. "Don't you speak to me of the Lord!"

She drew back and Josh leaned forward, his tone gentle now. "Easy, now. You think about her request, Dyson. I'll be back at the end of the day."

"Don't speak to me of the Lord," he repeated. The restless repetition continued long into the afternoon. The doctor's demanding litany bellowed from the wagon during suppertime, disturbing the meal and upsetting the women. Sometimes he yelled and sometimes he whispered, but always the refrain was the same. "Don't speak to me of the Lord."

Concerned mothers covered small children's ears and

hurried them back to the privacy of their wagons to eat while the men lingered in small groups. As Copper washed dishes, she listened to the talk.

"I buried three Kiowas," one man said.

"I didn't touch the savages," someone else muttered.

The first speaker stared straight ahead. "A man ought to have a grave."

"Those heathens bury their own differently than we do. Some are put on scaffolds. Why, I've even seen 'em hanging in trees. Some are buried in caves, others in graves. Those cold-blooded killers are a superstitious lot. I've seen 'em bury a warrior and then destroy his horse and everything he owned in an effort to provide help in the next life."

"Don't matter." The other man said, "I buried these in the ground, but after putting three of those savages in their graves I quit. Redlin was foolish enough to dig one for the woman."

"A waste of time and energy. There'll be no one here to put her in it."

The men's conversation faded as Copper hung a dishtowel to dry, and then went to sit with a group of women near the fire.

"Understand Mike will be taking you back in the morning," Adele said as she patted the seat beside her. "It's not going to be the same around here without you, honey."

Copper took a seat and warmed her hands. "Dr. Dyson's in no shape to help." She sighed. "I'll miss everyone too, especially the children and our noon lessons."

"Who would ever have thought this would happen?" Lil held little Carrie on her lap. The child's eyes drooped.

Yes, who would have thought this would ever happen. Copper closed her eyes, recalling the pain she had undergone, only to meet with this destiny.

"Just doesn't seem right, but I've lived long enough to know life can turn on you in a minute. Can't really blame the good doctor. A body can stand only so much."

Copper opened her eyes and murmured. "Well, will you look at that."

Eyes turned to follow her direction. An unsteady Dyson stood in the canvas opening of Adele's wagon. Grizzled, disheveled, and looking more like fifty miles of bad road instead of Copper's redemption, there he stood, big as life.

He met the women's stares. "Don't just sit there; get me some strong black coffee."

Chapter 18

Clouds skittered across a cold moon. Anxiety settled over the camp as women carried coffee to Dyson. Refusing food, he took the coffee and let the flap down. Talk once again centered on the fort and what lay ahead. All were relieved to be moving on come morning, but lingering concern tainted relief.

"Before we move on, I think Mike and Richardson ought to ride out and have one more look-see around." A man drew his wife closer to his side. "We're just as anxious to be on our way as the next person, but we want to be sure those Injuns ain't waiting to jump us somewhere on down the road."

Discussion erupted, and they took a vote. Caution won out. Mike and Richardson agreed to scout the area one last time before the wagons moved out.

Copper trailed Adele to the wagon, knowing that sleep would be long in coming tonight.

"Copper?"

She turned to see Redlin approaching. Adele continued to the wagon as the wagon master approached.

"Got time for a cup of coffee?"

"Yes. Is something on your mind?"

A weary smile surfaced. "Just feel the need for your companionship."

She smiled. Turmoil brought out the best in this man. "You heard Dyson has asked for coffee?"

"I heard, but don't read anything into the request. The man wants a drink, not coffee." They returned to the fire and Copper started toward the chuck wagon box. "Let me get that," Josh said, as he retrieved two cups. "You don't need to be taking any more steps than necessary." The considerate side of him was always close to the surface.

Copper made a place for him next to her. He handed her a cup and sat down. "You wanted the train to move on, didn't you?"

Nodding, she cupped the hot liquid in front of her face and breathed the fragrance. "Time's passing. I love these people, and I want them safely to their destination before heavy snow flies."

"Every day we sit brings us a day closer to worsening weather, but one more area search is wise. The red man is like the wind. Here one moment, gone the next."

She settled next to him, absorbing the warmth of his body, which, oddly enough, felt completely normal. "I understand."

His gaze fixed on the low-burning embers. "Do you?"

She glanced up. "Do I understand?" She wasn't sure she'd caught the meaning of his question.

"You don't think I'm making a mistake by not moving on quickly?"

"You? Misjudging a situation?" She sobered. "No, I trust your reasoning. Better safe than sorry. Isn't that what they say?"

He glanced at her, and amusement hovered at the corners of his mouth. "Well, great day in the morning. We are making progress."

Her features sobered. "The Indian woman hasn't passed?"

He shook his head, then removed his hat and laid it on the ground. "I hate to leave her, but I'm responsible for many more lives. She can't last. She hasn't eaten or taken water for who knows how long."

"You hesitate to leave her? You can say that after what you've just witnessed?"

"I believe it's likely that she was a captive, and unless I miss my guess, she is Kiowa. Could be that she was caught up in a fight she didn't initiate. Maybe the savages didn't realize she was here." Shaking his head, he admitted. "Hard to say. Could be she wasn't captive, that she was only trying to join her family on a reservation. There's a lot of tribes being forced to government land. Family ties are strong among these people. No one will ever know what happened." He fell silent, then observed, "Makes you wonder how long it will be before all the Indians are on reservations."

Suddenly Josh's hand went to his holster. Copper set her cup aside and listened. Nothing but the crackling fire met her ears.

"What?"

"Quiet." Josh eased to his feet, his gaze scanning the camp's perimeter. Alert now, the two watched a horse emerge from the shadows. The rider was an Indian wearing a breechclout and thigh-length buckskin leggings. He carried a lance pointed down at the ground. Decorated with beads and feathers, it had a white flag attached to the tip.

Copper eased closer to Josh until she crowded him.

"Easy," he cautioned.

Her heart wedged in her throat. "How many are there?"

Uncertainty invaded her thoughts. Was this savage part of the same band that had attacked the fort earlier? Had he returned to make another kill?

The Kiowa walked the horse into camp. The men's eyes locked while hysteria rose to the back of Copper's throat.

The red man reined up. He sat in the middle of the corral, eyes fixed on the wagon master.

"Stay here." Josh moved to meet the newcomer.

She caught him back. "You can't go out there!"

"Stay here," he repeated. "And don't make a sound."

He eased her aside and slowly walked to the war pony. Copper focused on the Colt strapped to his thigh. He wasn't defenseless, but how fast could he draw if the Indian moved first?

Copper held her breath when the Kiowa spoke first. From this distance, she could distinguish that he spoke perfect English.

Josh paused twenty feet away. "You speak English?"

The man nodded.

The two men exchanged a few brief sentences. Though she couldn't hear the entire text, the conversation appeared to be nonthreatening in tone. Copper resisted the urge to awaken the camp; Josh had said to remain quiet, but every nerve in her wanted to scream.

The warrior reined his animal around, and the horse walked out of camp.

Copper bolted to meet Josh. "What was that about?"

"He says the woman is his mother."

"The dying woman?"

He nodded. "He's asked permission to remain with her until she passes."

"You're not serious." Her gaze traced the line of thicket.

Grim-faced, Josh nodded. "As serious as death."

"You're not going to grant him permission, are you?" After what they'd witnessed, she couldn't imagine the savage would have the gall to come here and ask such a thing. This could be a farce, a trap to snare them all into certain death.

Rubbing a hand across his unshaven face, Josh admitted, "I don't know. I have to think about it."

"You have to *think* about it? You can't be serious! Why, the folks on this train will never permit it!"

"Blessed are the peacemakers, for they shall be called sons of God."

Disbelief came out in a whoosh. "Don't quote Scripture at a time like this." She couldn't imagine him even considering the request.

"It's late." He turned and emptied his cup onto the fire. "You need your rest. As soon as Richardson says it's safe, we'll pull out. I'll stop by your wagon and say good-bye."

"Josh." She caught his arm, her eyes imploring him. "You can't be serious. How do we know he isn't setting us up for another raid?"

"I don't know that."

"You can't put this train in further danger."

"I'm aware of my responsibilities, Copper. Let me handle this."

She couldn't. She couldn't let his overwhelming compassion trump conventional sense. "You have to put this to a vote. Do you realize what you are risking if you allow this?"

"Yes. And I realize what this man risked when he rode in here. The woman is his mother. And there is a chance that out there in the brush a daughter is waiting. The Kiowa women are close. All he wants is respect for his dying parent."

"*If* she is his mother."

"If," he conceded.

"It could be a trick."

"It could be," he acknowledged.

His words sank in. She glanced at the darkness outside the circle of wagons and thought about her mother. How she wished she'd had a few minutes alone with her before that ship sank. "Do you really think that woman is his mother?"

He shrugged. "He claims he wasn't part of the marauding band, but he knew she was being held here. Word has spread about the raid, and he came to ask for her body. When I told him that she was alive he asked to be with her until her death."

The gravity of the situation threatened to undo her. Did Josh trust this heathen's word enough to grant him last moments with his mother? To risk endangering the whole wagon train? Or would he turn the man away? She sighed. "This is just plain wretched. We're cursed if we do and cursed if we don't."

"Or just plain cursed," he agreed.

Blessed are the peacemakers. But the Lord gave men common sense.

Their gazes met, and she succumbed to his empathy.

"Oh Josh. What will we do?"

"We?"

She looked away. "If you tell the others they will surely turn him away."

"They surely will, and I have to decide if I can live with that or if I put my trust in a son's word." His gaze locked with hers. "What would you have me to do?"

She was both flattered and aghast that he would ask her opinion. She wasn't equipped to make such a monumental decision. Her heart said let the man be with his mother in her dying hours, but sanity told her the Kiowa could be using this as diversion while they organized for another attack.

"I can't choose. I'm not wise enough."

He nodded. "Nor am I. The Comanche are tight with the Kiowa. That much I do know. There could be hundreds of them setting out there waiting for the right moment to swoop down on us."

Suddenly the silence seemed deafening. Behind the row of trees sat a son. Perhaps a daughter. Waiting.

Or perhaps hundreds of savages with a thirst for blood.

This brave was waiting to mourn or waiting to kill. Which was it?

Behind the fort wall a woman, maybe a mother, lay near death, alone, without her people. Christianity, being Christ-like, involved more than words. She knew the Indians put their trust in many things . . . rocks, animals, the wind, the Great Spirit. The problem was that Josh didn't know this particular warrior's beliefs, and one mistake could doom the whole wagon train. Did the fact that he spoke English make him more trustworthy?

Josh turned and walked away. Her eyes followed him as he went to the side of Adele's wagon and paused. *He was praying.* The realization sank in. As firm as he could be at times, he believed in a higher source. A man of his strong convictions would seem more at home in a pulpit than leading a wagon train.

The moon crept higher in the sky. Cold wind buffeted the circled wagons.

Finally, Josh returned to the fire where she stood waiting. "I'm going to let him go to her."

Fear struggled with pride within her. She knew in her heart of hearts that this was the right decision, but she also knew the significance of this decision was weighing like an anchor in Josh's mind.

"May I come with you?"

He nodded. "I'm going to get Richardson and a few men up and armed in case this turns out to be an ambush."

"Oh Josh . . ."

He shook his head. "We'll know soon enough. I may be crazy, but I see a hurting son. I may pay a price for my error."

Or the whole train might.

With a sigh, Copper said, "Let's hope God's got his eye on you right now."

Walking their horses, the three riders approached the fort. Even though the slow pace would seem to indicate nothing but a peaceful purpose, Josh called out, "Friend."

The two guards lowered their guns. "Josh?" Doug Millet frowned. "You should be asleep this time of—" When the man spotted the Kiowa, his rifle shot to his shoulder.

"Let him pass!"

"Pass? Redlin, have you lost your mind?" Doug steadied the rifle. "He's one of them."

The redskin spoke. "I bear you no harm."

"Lower your gun," Josh said, in a tone that had the authority of a rifle shot.

The guard slowly lowered the hammer on his rifle, but he kept it firmly fixed to his shoulder.

Josh led the small party through the gate. The animals paused in front of the office and the riders dismounted.

Carrying a lantern, Redlin led the party to a figure lying on a pallet near a fire. Sadie sat nearby.

Kneeling, the savage reached for the woman's hand.

The dying woman opened her eyes, and awareness filled the dark brown recesses. She spoke softly in her native tongue.

The man answered her.

Closing her eyes, she tightly gripped his hand.

Sadie eased closer to Copper. "What's going on?"

"This man is her son."

"Her son." Sadie closed her eyes. "Merciful God. She's been holding on for some reason. Good Lord knows how she's lasted this long."

The Kiowa held to her hand, his eyes focused on the frail figure. He glanced up to meet Redlin's gaze. "May I have some room?"

Nodding, Josh motioned for the group to move back.

Somehow, at that moment, the man seemed more individual and less Kiowa. He lifted his face to the heavens and spoke in a strong baritone. "Great Spirit. I ask that you have patience. This woman is good. She has not harmed others. She has walked in the paths of peace. Give her life. If this cannot be, then I ask that you travel with her in her journey."

Wind whistled through the cracks in the wall. The scene was surreal; a lone savage kneeling beside his dying mother but surrounded by men who, on the whole, were more interested in killing him than understanding his grief. What must the great Creator think of such senseless tragedy?

Moments passed. The son held his mother's hand. Finally, she opened her eyes and smiled at him.

Copper turned away when she saw tears rolling from the corners of the son's lids.

Lifting one hand, the mother gently wiped away his tears, whispering softly. Somehow, Copper knew she was saying good-bye, expressing her love. A mother's love for a devoted son.

Copper glanced at Josh. She was so proud of him. The decision had not been an easy one, and when others learned of what he'd done he would be accused of reckless behavior, but she would accuse him only of fully comprehending the meaning of love. She knew he'd made the right decision. She hoped that when her Creator called her there would be a man like Josh Redlin nearby.

With a simple sigh, the woman closed her eyes and stepped to the beyond.

Stoic now, the son gently placed her hands together and rested his face on her chest, shoulders heaving.

After a moment, he rose. "I may take my mother's body?"

Josh nodded. "I'll help you."

"No. I will carry my mother." He collected a small bundle of her clothes and a leather medicine sack. Then he wrapped her snugly in a warm blanket, scooped her into his arms, and carried her out the charred window. He laid her across his pony in front of him and climbed onto its back. Reining the animal, the son met Redlin's gaze. "Thank you, Josh Redlin."

Josh nodded. "Go in peace."

The Indian walked his animal to the gate and then rode off.

Copper swiped at her eyes. "What was that all about? Why did he take her out of the window?"

"It's the Kiowa way. By taking her out of the window he hopes to keep her soul from returning to this place."

"Where will he take her?"

"Somewhere in the hills. He'll find a rocky crevice and bury her there."

Josh nodded to Sadie and Copper. "Ladies. It's very late. You should be in bed."

Sadie rode Copper's horse, and Copper rode behind Josh as they returned to the camp. Copper considered all the unique days in her life, but this one had to be the most distinctive. Today she had learned what it was to truly be Christ-like.

Tonight had brought God home in a way she would never forget. How could she ever fully understand the blending of religions and culture that formed the beliefs of this Kiowa brave?

Dr. Dyson's sudden resurrection appeared even more promising by daybreak. He asked for bacon and eggs. When told of the progress, Josh once again delayed departure until noon. By late morning, Dyson ordered Redlin to bring the woman with the wounded ankle to him. Shortly afterward, Copper sat down in Adele's rocking chair, and Dyson had his first look at her injury.

His eyes told the story, but he didn't immediately seal her doom. "It's bad."

Copper released a pent-up sigh. She'd traveled all this way to have him tell her what she already knew? "Then you can't do anything?"

"Even if I could work a miracle, I don't have my instruments."

An explanation wasn't needed; everyone who gathered in Adele's wagon knew the reason for the doctor's dilemma. The savages had destroyed or taken everything.

Josh shifted. "If we could provide what you need, or at least some of it, could you help?"

The doctor's hand visibly shook when he gently probed the injury. He confirmed what Copper had feared. "The damage has started to mend." Then he spoke softly, more to himself than to the others. "I don't know." He paused and dropped his face into his hands. "I just don't know."

Those gathered waited until he regained his composure. Finally he looked up. "Look at my hands; they're shaking like a leaf in a storm. Even if I decide to operate, I can't do it without a drink."

Copper glanced at Josh and he shook his head. The man had come too far down the road of sobriety to be allowed to go back to the bottle.

The wagon master shook his head. "We don't have liquor."

"I need a drink," the doctor contended. He held out his

hands. "Look at these. Under ideal conditions I would operate, but not like this."

"Give him a drink," Sadie implored.

Josh shook his head. "It isn't a matter of judgment. I've checked. There's no liquor in camp. We didn't have much, and the emotional toll of what the men have seen since we got here has depleted the supply."

"Don't give me that," Dyson scoffed. "Every train carries a supply."

"Not this one. Not until we pass a town where we can replenish our stock."

Strained silence filled the wagon. Finally the doctor surrendered. From some deep reservoir of humanity, compassion, and medical training came the decision. "I'll do what I can."

The entire group let out a simultaneous sigh of relief. Copper dropped her face in her hands and tried to absorb the meaning of the reprieve, however tentative. Josh's fingers pressed into her shoulder. "Tell me what you need."

"I'll need light, all the light possible." Dyson listed additional items and Josh nodded.

Pandemonium erupted as the order went out for makeshift medical implements.

Adele set water to boil, then stripped the pallet and put on clean sheets while Sadie washed and prepared Copper's leg for surgery.

Dr. Dyson stood in the bed of the wagon, watching the assembly.

"You've lost your faith, haven't you?" Copper spoke softly from her place in the wagon. Somehow she sensed that pious platitudes were the last thing the man needed.

He mutely shook his head. She wasn't sure if he was disagreeing or simply couldn't face his conclusions.

As the implements were gathered, Josh stepped inside the wagon. He knelt before Copper, who sat in the rocker. "This is the big moment."

"The biggest," she said. "Hope is a wonderful thing."

He nodded, his eyes lending her much-needed strength.

"The train must leave early morning. We can't delay any longer. Weather's going to be closing in on us."

She frowned. "You're leaving me?"

"Richardson's taking the wagons ahead. I'll catch up in a few days."

She smiled. "Then Mike won't be taking me back?"

"No, I'll be taking you back."

"Are you ready, Miss Wilson?" Dr. Dyson's voice broke into her sudden giddiness. Josh was staying behind to be with her. She was up to any challenge.

They moved her pallet to the back of the wagon, where the late afternoon sun would give the best light. Then Copper moved from her rocker to the pallet that would serve as an operating table.

Dr. Dyson picked up a knife, held the instrument to the light, and then dipped the blade in a pan of steaming water. "If you haven't got the stomach for this, Redlin, you best step way back."

Josh nodded. "I'll be close."

Adele stood at Copper's head, ready to keep her firmly in place. Josh bent and kissed Copper, then straightened and moved away. His eyes met the doctor's. "How long?"

Dyson shook his head. "As long as it takes."

Nodding, he walked a distance away and stood.

The doctor's eyes met Copper's, and she saw both doubt and resolve there. He squeezed some laudanum into her mouth.

"I'm sorry, but this won't be enough to kill all the pain. It is the best we have. Even a simple whiskey would help me, but if we're to believe Redlin, there is none available. I had a small supply of opium but the Kiowa took it."

She nodded. "If there were whiskey available I'd let you have it. Honest. I'm strong. I can take anything." She flashed a smile, wishing she really felt as strong as she was trying to sound. "I can endure the surgery if you can make me walk again."

"My good lady. I am not your Maker."

"No . . . of course not. I just wanted you to know you don't have to worry about me screaming or anything. I won't. I'm strong."

"Mmm. Yes, well, let's get started."

He inclined his head to Adele. The last thing Copper remembered was Dyson's grim invocation. "May God have mercy on your soul."

Chapter 19

⌒

Josh Redlin's face, then Adele's studious expression. Then Josh again. Faces drifted in and out of Copper's wavering sight.

"Come on, honey. Wake up."

She didn't want to wake up; she preferred to stay in the blissful black void. Still, Sadie's anxious whispers penetrated her desire to remain in the nothingness.

"The Almighty was merciful. The poor thing couldn't have made it through the surgery without his intervening."

"Aye," Adele murmured. "With only that little bit of medicine, the fainting was the best thing that could've happened to her."

Faint? Had she fainted? When she'd vowed to be so wholly courageous?

Sadie and Adele spoke in unison.

"How is she, Doctor?"

"Were you able to help her?"

Then Josh's tense voice. "Copper? Can you hear me?"

Dr. Dyson's voice penetrated the fog. "Folks, I'd like a word alone with Miss Wilson."

The two women clucked and cooed to the patient but obediently drifted away. She felt Josh's presence remain. "Mr. Redlin?"

Head clearing, Copper gritted her teeth against the white-hot pain that was radiating up her leg from her ankle. "He can stay." She reached for his hand.

"Miss Wilson, you might want to hear what I have to say in private."

"No." Copper swallowed against a dry throat. "He can hear anything you have to tell me."

The doctor washed his hands in the water basin. "If that's what you want."

Josh moved closer, his eyes pools of concern.

Dropping into the rocker, the doctor rubbed his temples. "I fear I could do little to help."

Copper thought the words would bring even more agony, but oddly enough, the diagnosis brought peace. She had done all that was possible to avert this moment, and God's answer was "No." Josh squeezed her hand.

"I may have helped somewhat," Dyson corrected. "The way the ankle was you would have been consigned to a crutch for the rest of your life. Now, with God's grace, when the incision heals the ankle will be as strong as it is ever going to get. But I can't predict how good that will be."

Copper noticed that the doctor now spoke of God's mercy. Perhaps he would heal too. "I may not have to use a crutch?"

"We won't know for a few weeks, but I believe I was able

to set the bone so that only a slight limp, if anything, will hinder you." He rested his head on the back of the rocker, staring at the roof of the wagon. "I wish I could have done more, but you're fortunate the bone didn't break the skin. You would have lost the foot."

Josh's hand tightened in hers when she spoke. "Thank you, Doctor. The assessment is far better than I had feared."

She might have a limp for the rest of her life . . . but there was still a touch of hope. Copper closed her eyes.

"I'll get you a cup of coffee, Doctor." Josh left the wagon and the doctor remained in the rocker, eyes closed. His gray features were drained. Copper reached over and took his hand and held it.

Tears rolled from the corners of his eyes.

"Can you talk about it yet?" she asked softly. For the man bore an unspeakable weight. Perhaps if he spoke of his great loss he would be able to go on and eventually find his purpose again. And she welcomed the opportunity to think about something other than her pain.

He was silent for so long she thought he'd rejected her invitation. She tightened her hold on his hand, a surgeon's hand. She wanted to wipe away the tears that coursed down his weathered features. She tried willing him to speak, shutting out her hurt. His face contorted, and he said, "Did Redlin tell you where he found me?"

"In your office?"

His mirthless laugh stunned her. "In the root cellar. He was good enough to cover for me that day."

"Root cellar?"

"Drunk. While my wife and child were being slaughtered, I laid in the root cellar drunk, swigging gin." The enormity of his admission stunned her. He was opening his soul to her. A part of her didn't want to hear any more, but the words came out, one upon one, hopeless admissions.

"Word was the Kiowa were on the prowl and everyone was uneasy, perhaps even frightened. Mary, my youngest daughter, had been poorly for several days. Then the day before the raid she died. She was only two years old. She had the same big brown eyes and dark brown hair of her mother. I don't know what happened. Within two days she went from being tired and having a low fever to death. I should have been able to do something. I should have saved her. I'm a doctor and I couldn't keep my own daughter from dying.

"It hit me hard. My wife never said it was my fault, but I could see in her eyes that she felt that I could have done something, something beyond my ability." He opened his eyes and met hers. "Mary died about dawn and we buried her that afternoon. I sought release the only way I knew how: in the bottle. After the funeral I grabbed all the whiskey I could carry and headed for the root cellar. I couldn't face my wife and I couldn't bear to look at Sally, my other daughter. By dusk I was in a stupor.

"The Kiowa hit us the next day, but I was totally unaware of it until it was over. Miss Wilson, I'm not proud of my actions, but sometimes a man copes the best he knows how, and gin was the only way I could face life that day. That's where your Redlin found me. During the battle I was drunk, oblivious to what was going on above me. That's the only reason my life was spared. Those redskins didn't think to look for a drunken doctor lying in the darkest corner of the root cellar." His features crumpled and he broke, his shoulders heaving with such grief, Copper feared he might never regain composure. She was so taken aback by the horror, she couldn't find words. For the remainder of his life, this was the knowledge this man would carry.

Heaving with emotion, his voice came through sobs. "I don't want to live anymore. I've had a drinking problem for many years. Ginny hated it. When she could, she'd steal my bottles and pour them onto the ground, but I'd just get another from one of the men." He shook his head. "Why did you bring me back? Is this my punishment, to live with this nightmare the rest of my days? I lost the woman I love and two precious daughters because of the bottle. I should have been up here fighting for my family, for my company. Instead I was drowning my weaknesses in a bottle of whiskey."

By now Josh stood in the doorway holding a cup of steaming coffee. He'd heard most of the confession. What must a man with Redlin's grit think of such an act?

Coward. The offensive tag didn't fit Dale Dyson. A coward didn't drag himself from self-pity and remorse to make an effort to possibly save a young woman from becoming a cripple when all he wanted to do was die. Yet Copper well understood the man's agony. He had succumbed to human frailty while his family fought for their lives. How could he ever forgive himself?

Josh moved to put the cup of coffee in Dyson's hand. The doctor stared at the contents, obviously reliving that tragic day.

"I didn't hear a thing. Not one gunshot. That night I staggered out of the cellar intent on cleaning up and going home to a hot supper, and then I saw—" He broke off. "I found my wife and daughter and buried them next to Mary. Then I returned to the cellar, and I don't remember anything until you found me, Redlin. No, that's not true. At one point I tried to take my life; I recall making a noose. I looked for a gun, but all I found was a piece of rope. It was so old and my fingers were so stiff that I couldn't get it tied so that it would hold my weight. I couldn't even take my life. I'm not a man; I'm a disgrace."

During his confession, Josh remained silent. Now he said quietly, "A man isn't measured by his acts; he's measured by the Creator."

"What kind of Creator would allow a man to do what I did?"

"God's ways are sometimes mysterious. You are certainly not the first man to fail in a crisis. The apostle Peter comes to mind."

Dyson stared at his coffee. "You don't know, Redlin. You can't know what it's like to lose everything you love and know that you might have been able to prevent their deaths."

"A lot of lives were lost in that attack. If you had been seen, you would have suffered the same fate."

Dyson's features crumpled. "Don't you think I know that? Don't you think I wish it had happened that way? My prayer is that God will take me today, rather than let me stay in this . . . this . . . hell that I'm in now."

Redlin met the doctor's eyes. "Every man has a purpose. Who knows your purpose, but it wasn't your time the day of the attack."

"If nothing more, you were spared to prevent me from using a crutch the rest of my life," Copper reasoned.

"Words. Nothing but words." Dyson spat them rather than

said them. He set the cup beside the rocker. "I'll never take another breath that I don't remember what I've done to my wife and children. I have no right to be here, no right at all, and I curse the day you people brought me back to face my disgrace."

He stood up, swaying with fatigue. "Stay off the foot completely, Miss Wilson."

"How long?"

"Six weeks at least. Then have a doctor check the results. He may want you off the ankle longer. Do what he says."

"I will. Thank you."

He dismissed her gratitude with a shake of his head. "There's still a chance of infection from the surgery, but the wound is clean. I wish I'd had whiskey for more than one reason, but you shouldn't have any trouble." He turned and left the wagon.

Josh bent to kiss Copper. Their eyes met and he smiled. "Get some sleep. We have had better news than we feared."

"Thank you for staying with me." She gently reached to touch the tip of his nose. "You give me comfort."

The expression in his eyes told her they both gave each other something; something both needed. She was becoming important to him. That was the greatest gift of this day.

Their gazes held, she drinking in his strength. "My heart goes out to Dr. Dyson. Can you imagine carrying such a burden?"

"I know that man is often tested far beyond what he believes that he can stand. But he goes on." His eyes turned distant, as though he was recalling his trials. "Somehow, he goes on. Dyson will make it, but his life will never be the same." He straightened. "I'll be back shortly. I want to speak to Dyson alone." A man-to-man thing. Copper hoped that in some measure, Josh would be able to help the doctor.

Later Adele and Sadie sat with her for a while, and then the doctor returned to sleep in the rocker by her side.

Copper heard the camp settling for the night. A light wind ruffled the canvas. She knew the doctor, though weary, couldn't rest. His heart was with the occupants of three shallow graves that lay within the fort, and the many others surrounding them.

"You can't blame yourself." She spoke into the darkness, not even sure that he heard her. "We're all imperfect beings."

How many times had she recklessly done things for which, but for the mercy of God, she would have paid a tremendous penalty? The doctor's voice broke into her thoughts. "Do you ever wonder why God does what he does?"

She smiled into the darkness. "Every day."

"Nothing makes sense, you know."

"Is it supposed to?"

He didn't answer, and she let him come to his conclusions. She wasn't a theologian. She could barely remember the Scripture she'd learned over the years, but its meaning was etched in her heart, and the way she had it figured, a body had two choices: believe in a higher source, or not believe in anything.

Two choices. Even odds on getting the meaning of life right. She saw a higher source when she looked at the stars as numerous as Abraham's descendants. She understood that new life was resurrected every spring in the trees, bushes, and grass. She chose trust and belief.

She could be wrong.

Then again, she could be right.

Perfect peace or imperfect turmoil. The choice was a stark one, with no ground in between. She prayed the good doctor would reach the same conclusion, for without personal peace life didn't make a lick of sense.

By seven forty-five the following morning the wagons were hitched and ready to roll. Saying good-bye to Adele and Sadie was harder than Copper had imagined.

Adele bent and hugged Copper, who had been transferred to a pallet next to the fire. Josh, the doctor, and Copper would remain another day, and then Josh would return Copper to Thunder Ridge before he rejoined the train somewhere on down the trail.

"This don't mean we can't write." The older woman sniffed. "I expect to hear from you once a month, and you say hello to Willow and Audrey. I want to hear from them too."

Sadie squeezed between the fire and Adele. "Same goes for me."

"I promise." Copper bit back tears, determined to keep this parting on a happy note. They'd come a long way together, sacrificed much, and tolerated even more. This should be a time of celebration, though the wagon train would face many more hardships before they reached Colorado Springs. Copper only had five, possibly six days' ride, and she would be home. Home! Thunder Ridge or Beeder's Cove? It really didn't matter as long as it was close to Audrey and Willow.

If she was lucky, Beeder's Cove school board would hold the teaching position until next fall. Whoever had filled in during her absence would maybe be moved to Blackberry Hill. By then her injury should be completely healed.

Redlin called from the distance. "It's time, ladies." In the background, Richardson's "Wagons roll!" filtered down the line of waiting rigs.

One last hug, and Sadie and Adele said good-bye. Copper knew most likely she'd never see the two wonderful souls again this side of heaven. Colorado Springs was a long way from Beeder's Cove.

The last wagon rumbled off and faded into the distance. Copper listened to the men's whistles controlling the stock, the protesting of the cows, and the squeak of wagon wheels. She realized she was blinking back tears.

Josh knelt beside her pallet. "Hey, no tears allowed. Colorado isn't that far off."

"It might as well be eternity."

He reached out and tugged her right cheek. "Not by rail. The railroads are building all through these parts. It won't be long before you can board a rail car and travel to Colorado in no time at all."

The thought was a lovely one, but Copper couldn't imagine the luxury. Forgo dust, Indians, and rough roads and sit in a railroad car and be whisked to your destination in a matter of days? Only the very rich could afford the privilege.

That evening the campfire burned low. Three of the best horses grazed nearby. The setting was surreal; her and two men. Beyond the light, Fort Riceson's ghostly presence loomed like a bad nightmare.

Josh had kept busy most of the day preparing for the ride back to Thunder Ridge. Over a cold supper, he approached the subject Copper had been afraid to voice: What were Dyson's plans? They couldn't just ride off and leave him here, yet he hadn't mentioned a word about joining them.

Redlin tossed coffee remains in the fire. "What about you, Doctor?"

The man glanced up. "What about me?"

"What's your plan? You can't stay here."

Dyson turned back to stare at the fire. "I haven't any plans."

"You can't sit here," Josh said. "Come with us."

"To Thunder Ridge?"

"It's a nice town." He glanced at Copper and winked. "A man could lay down roots there."

Dyson shook his head. "My roots are lying in that fort."

"In time, you'll plant new ones." Josh's tone gentled. "I'm not suggesting it will be easy, but there's nothing here any longer. Ride back with us, at least until you get on your feet again."

"I'm still a member of the cavalry. I have to report somewhere."

"I understand. Do your superiors know that you survived the attack?"

The doctor shook his head. "I've spoken to no one."

Copper doubted news of the attack had reached the government yet. Information was slow to come in these parts.

"Please." Copper added her invitation. "Come with us. Once you're in Thunder Ridge you can notify your superiors and resume your duties. We can't ride off and leave you here."

To leave the doctor sitting and grieving alone at the graves of his family was unthinkable.

Dyson stared sightlessly into the fire. Copper didn't know if a word they said reached him, but they couldn't desert him. If they must, Josh would have to truss him up like a Christmas goose and tie him to the horse.

"You're coming with us," she announced.

The doctor neither accepted nor rejected her statement.

By sunup, Josh lifted Copper onto the saddle and elevated her foot in a makeshift sling alongside the horse's neck. The supply of laudanum was very low, so this journey was not likely to be a pleasant one. The long-anticipated trip home was not one she was looking forward to.

Her eyes scanned the area. Dale Dyson was nowhere in sight. "Is he coming?"

Josh tightened a cinch. "I haven't seen him this morning. He was gone when I woke up."

She located the third horse still grazing nearby. "Is he in the fort?"

"Don't know." He moved to check his saddlebags. "A man has a right to privacy, Copper. We invited him to come; it's up to him whether he accepts help or not. The doctor's carrying a heavy weight; you have to understand that."

Copper longed to ride to the fort, where instinct told her Dyson stood in front of three fresh graves. Yet Josh's words rang true. A man was entitled to his privacy—his life. Only the good Lord had a say on the doctor's future.

Josh glanced her way. "Weather's good. We'll take it easy; if your pain gets to be too much, you're to tell me and we'll stop."

"I will. I promise." But she wanted to get home. Quickly. She could stand pain. She'd lived with it long enough.

"When you need to rest, whistle."

She nodded, her gaze drifting back to the fort. "Shouldn't we go check on the doctor? Maybe he intends to come and time had gotten away from him. We should say good-bye."

Josh shook his head and then swung into his saddle. "He knows the time."

Nodding, Copper reined the horse and fell in behind the big stallion, her eyes fixed on the fort's open double gates. *Please let him come, God. You can't leave him out here grieving all alone.*

Josh turned to glance over his shoulder. "A man has to do what he has to do."

"I can't bear to leave him."

"You do what you have to do."

She set the horse into an easy gait and forced her thoughts away from the pain in her ankle to home. Home. Willow, Audrey. Pleasant memories. She'd had her fill of sorrow.

Half a mile down the road she whirled, breaking into a grin when she heard approaching hoofbeats. Dr. Dyson's animal covered the distance and drew even with her mare. Josh glanced over and nodded. "Good to see you, Dyson."

Dyson fixed his eyes on the road and acknowledged the wagon master. "Redlin."

Copper smiled. "I was so afraid that you weren't coming."

"I wasn't. Then I realized the Kiowa took away a lot of things, but they didn't take away my oath to serve mankind. I'll ride to Thunder Ridge, keep an eye on that injury, and then rejoin a unit."

Josh smiled. "Sounds good."

Nudging her horse, Copper set off for Thunder Ridge with more joy in her heart than she had experienced in weeks. *Thank you, God.*

She didn't need any more prayer than that. She didn't

need to mention specific blessings. The good Lord knew she was grateful that she didn't have to leave the stricken doctor behind.

Thunder Ridge wouldn't restore Dyson's will to live, or bring back his wife and daughters, but Fort Riceson certainly held no future.

The past was buried and the future lay ahead.

Chapter 20

"Ouch!"

"Just stay put and this will be over quickly."

"That's what you say every time, and it just gets worse. Owhh! Must you use that vile concoction?"

Audrey briskly rubbed the whiskey and salt mixture into Copper's backside. "Jolie says there's nothing better to relieve soreness and keep the rash from getting infected. This would not be an ideal area to get infected, you know." She dipped the cloth in the pan of liquid and reapplied the poultice.

"Oh mother of—" Copper howled. She did not appreciate the humor in Audrey's anatomical reference about rash.

Willow sat in the bedroom chair offering advice. "You should have never ridden so long and hard."

Gritting her teeth, Copper endured the treatment. She should be used to it by now. She, Redlin, and Dyson arrived in Thunder Ridge last night after a grueling five-day ordeal. Their pace had been slow, but steady. The men stopped more often than she asked; they had been perfect escorts, but the last day her posterior hurt so badly that she almost forgot about the painful ankle. All in all, the ride home had cost her dearly. Months without having ridden a horse had left her backside vulnerable and now she was paying the price.

"Perhaps if you'd been where I thought you were you could have lessened my agony."

"Sorry about that, but everything happened so quickly. The schoolhouse fire and the ankle injury caught us all off guard. You were barely conscious when they whisked you off to see Dr. Dyson." Willow glanced at Audrey. "The last you knew Judge Madison's house was going to be auctioned the next day, and it was."

Copper half sat up. "Did it sell?" She couldn't imagine anyone actually wanting to buy the strange-looking house with its comical stovepipe construction, but she fully expected the pretentious banker's wife, Cordelia Padget, to nab it. It was the biggest house in town.

"Oh, it sold, all right." Audrey and Willow exchanged looks.

Sitting up straight, Copper squinted. "What's going on with you two?"

"Nothing." Audrey pushed her down and slapped another poultice on her backside. "An out-of-state buyer bought the place, much to Cordelia's dismay. The banker's wife was so certain that she and Horace were the only people around with enough money to obtain the house, but did she ever get a surprise."

Copper shifted. "Who bought it?"

Shrugging, Audrey dipped the cloth in a water basin. "Just a man from out of state, and he requested that Tucker and Willow remain here until he decided to settle down."

"Strange. Who in their right mind would want to live here? I mean, I've grown to love the town, but you'd have to live here for a spell before you acclimated to the climate."

Willow grinned. "True, and I'm sure the new owner plans to eventually settle here, but for the time being Tucker and I are more than happy to enjoy the extra space. The owner is allowing us free rent in exchange for taking care of the place." She sighed. "If we'd had to move into Tucker's one-room cabin we'd be mighty cramped for space."

Copper winced. "Especially with me turning back up on your doorstep. And I was so happy to settle in Beeder's Cove. The Widow Potts provided a lovely room."

Audrey wrung out the cloth. "You? What about me? I would have been forced to rent one of the Widow Gleeson's rooms, and while the woman is most pleasant, I would have missed being with Willow, and Tate certainly wouldn't have been able to run back and forth like he does."

"No, Eli's boy would have to find another cookie source," Willow teased. "But seriously, I don't know what I would have done without both your help during my confinement," she admitted. "Tucker is so good to me, but the mill takes up so much time. He can't sit with me all day. Oh, by the way, Copper. A letter from your Aunt Nancy came while you were gone."

"Aunt Nancy, in Ellsworth?"

"How many Aunt Nancys do you have? And exactly where is Ellsworth?"

"In Kansas, and from what Aunt Nancy writes the town is most boisterous. She says it attracts an army of ruffians, but Aunt Nancy is a bit of a hooligan herself." Copper had to laugh when she thought about the pint-sized lady. She hadn't seen her aunt in many long years.

Copper rested her head on the pillow. "Ellsworth. Now there would be an interesting town."

Willow tucked the envelope under Copper's pillow. "You must visit her someday."

"I should. She's invited me so many times since Mother passed. She was her only sister, you know. And Uncle Wilt passed away when he was very young. She moved to Kansas and never remarried."

"Dr. Dyson seems quite nice," Willow observed above Copper's misery. "Poor man—I wonder if he'll ever overcome his losses."

"Someday he will." Audrey straightened and wrung the cloth dry. "Look at Eli." A smile touched the corners of her mouth. "There was a time that I feared he would never get over losing his wife."

Willow met Copper's questioning gaze. "The two have been inseparable since you left. Honestly, I don't know how many picnics and long walks a body can take."

"You should talk." Audrey playfully punched Willow's shoulder. "I'm surprised you've even noticed." She turned to Copper and complained, "Newlyweds. A flaming buffalo could run through here and they wouldn't notice."

Copper buried her face in the pillowcase. She knew the feeling. When she was with Josh her surroundings disappeared. She'd learned many things on her brief trip to Fort Riceson, and one was that she'd misjudged Josh Redlin. The man was a prize, an anchor, a rock. Without him she was certain that she couldn't have made it through the long, tiresome journey and subsequent surgery and trip home.

She should have known that Willow and Audrey were completely attuned to her thoughts.

"So," Audrey prompted, "you and Redlin? What's with all the sudden niceness between you two?"

"What niceness?"

"Oh please." Willow laughed. "You two have bent over backward to be kind to one another. What happened on that trip that turned you from brawling street cats to . . . almost lovers?"

"I have no idea what you're talking about." Copper slowly sat up and eased her legs over the side of the bed. "Mr. Redlin and I have come to an understanding, but that doesn't mean that I like him and we agree on everything."

She didn't like him. She was in love with him. Madly in love. Dare she dream that he felt the same about her? He had been attentive during the surgery and the ride home, but he would have shown any woman the same courtesy. Josh was like that. Women flocked to him, and now she knew why. Yet in his eyes she might be little more than Milly Newsome personified.

Willow's tone dropped to conspiratorial. "Really? What's happened between you two?"

Sighing, Copper told them about the trip, the ups and downs and how she had come to love the maddening but oh-so-lovable wagon master, without whom life would have been intolerable these past weeks.

"You're in love with him?" Audrey shook her head. "Opposites do attract, but this seems rather like a copperhead and a skunk."

Copper's jaw firmed. "He's the best thing that's ever happened to me, Audrey Pride." She buttoned her pantaloons and carefully eased off the bed. "I don't know how I failed to recognize it in the beginning, but I fear now that he's seen enough of the real me he'll never fully return my affections." And yet he had kissed her. Had looked at her with . . . if not love, then most certainly great affection.

Audrey tugged Copper's nose. "Pish posh. We love you, and we have seen the *real* you."

Willow interrupted Copper's rebuttal. "Does Dr. Dyson intend to return to the cavalry?"

"Yes. He thought he'd report in when he got here, but we passed a post on the way home and he did so at the time. He requested that he remain with me until we know how the ankle is healing." Copper hobbled to a chair and gently eased down. Holding her right ankle aloft, she examined the bandage as she had every day since the operation.

"How long did you say it would be before you know if the doctor's efforts were successful?"

"Six to eight weeks."

"And the doctor is allowed to remain here in Thunder Ridge with you until then?"

"He could leave the cavalry any time he chooses. He's spent many long years in service, but I don't know what he will do. With his wife and family gone there'll be little to hold him anywhere."

"Does he have parents or siblings alive?"

"He hasn't said." Copper shook her head. "He says little, actually. It was only at the last minute that he decided to come with us. At first he said he was going to stay at the fort."

"You said nothing remained?"

"Nothing but graves and the horrible stench of death."

Audrey shook her head. "Eventually he would have been forced to leave."

"Josh and I feared he would do himself bodily harm if he remained behind, but a half mile down the road he caught up with us. Said he wanted to see his work through, but I imagine he knew that if he stayed it would be the last of him."

"Such a pity," Willow mused.

"Perhaps Eli can help." Audrey straightened the bedding.

Willow shook her head. "You know men; they don't talk it out like women do. They keep all their feelings inside until they explode."

Audrey turned pensive. "Not all men explode. Maybe they should. The release would allow healing to begin. Eli's kept his emotions for his wife buried so deep he wouldn't let himself feel—at least until lately." She sat down on the side of the bed. "He told me the other night he'd been afraid to look or even think about another woman since Genevieve's death because he felt he would be betraying her. He'd left her to fight in the war, and for her to die in childbirth having his son—that was betrayal enough."

"Perhaps the two men might console each other," Willow mused. "God works in mysterious ways."

"Indeed he does." Copper bent to tie her shoe. "How's Caleb's love life coming along?"

"Slow." Both Audrey and Willow giggled. "These days he seems a bit taken with Yvonne, but it is still too soon for her to consider marriage."

"Wasn't her deceased husband much older than her?"

"Very much older, and the union was based on need and respect, not love. At least not the exhilarating kind. Yvonne confessed that she loved him much as she would love a father. He had taken her in when her parents were slain by Indians."

"So it wasn't the giddy sort of love." Willow folded a hankie in her lap. "Perhaps in time something might have developed between the two."

Copper cast Willow a mischievous eye. "Of course there's always Meredith Johnson. I declare that young woman is man-hungry."

"Gray-hungry," Willow confirmed on a sour note. "She'd take any Gray, dead or alive."

Audrey's hands came to her hips. "Well, there's only one available. Eli's mine."

"So say you," Willow teased. "I don't see an engagement ring."

With a crafty grin, Audrey reached into her pocket, drew out a ring, and slipped it on the third finger of her left hand. Copper's and Willow's jaws simultaneously dropped.

Audrey good-naturedly wrinkled her nose. "He proposed last night. The ring belongs to his mother; it's a family heirloom. I've been waiting all day for the perfect time to tell you."

Pandemonium broke out as the women oohed and aahed over the token of intent.

"When?" Willow exclaimed. "When's the wedding?"

"A few months . . . at least until Eli can take some time off."

The three clasped one another in a long group hug. As delighted as Copper was with the news, she couldn't ignore the razor-sharp pain that sliced her heart to ribbons. She wanted Josh Redlin. She wanted a token of love. And yet Josh would ride out soon to rejoin the wagon train, and he'd made no mention of his intent toward her. Out of Thunder Ridge and possibly out of her life.

As thrilled as she was for Audrey and Eli, she couldn't break the melancholy that suddenly rendered her weepy.

On the way to the Madison home, Josh noticed that Dale Dyson had settled into Widow Gleeson's spare boarding room nicely. For three dollars a week he was assured a roof over his head and three hot meals a day. The widow kept two rooms for such occasions, but Thunder Ridge rarely had guests, so the good doctor had a comfortable deal and the privacy he craved. In time, Dyson's pain would ease. He'd never completely get over the loss, but if he stuck around Thunder Ridge, there were single women . . . The newly widowed Yvonne came to mind.

Five minutes later, Josh tapped on the door casing of Copper's bedroom door. They'd been back three days; he had to move on though his heart wasn't in the decision. She glanced up from the magazine she was reading. He flashed a grin. "Hello sleepyhead."

She returned the smile. "Did you stop by earlier?"

"An hour and a half ago."

She laid the magazine aside. "You should have had Audrey waken me. I've grown quite lazy of late."

"I figured you needed your rest. May I come in a minute?"

The moment she'd been dreading was here. She motioned him to a Queen Anne chair.

Removing his hat, he entered the room and sat down. "Staying off that foot, I see."

Nodding, she said, "I'm doing exactly as I'm told."

"I'll believe that when I see it." Their eyes met and they locked gazes. So much, and yet so little, was said in the brief exchange.

"You're leaving."

He nodded. "I can't delay any longer. The doctor is settled, you're on the mend." His features softened. "If there were a choice . . ."

"I know." He didn't have to say the words. They both knew he would be willing to stay, explore the feelings that were confusing, exhilarating, and useless. She knew so very little about him, and he knew everything about her. Not a promising state of affairs. Leaning closer, he picked up her hand. "I'll write."

She smiled, thinking about Susan. He'd have a lot of correspondence to complete.

"I'll answer."

"No." His hand tightened in hers. "I'll write, but it won't be possible for me to receive any returns. I should have the train safely to Colorado Springs sometime after the first of the year. Once I get them there, I'll come back. By then you should be up and around."

And then, what? Maybe they could pick up where they had left off. But exactly where had they left off? The relationship was as tenuous as it was promising.

He read the question in her eyes. "Been thinking of settling down here," he said, so quietly she wasn't sure she had heard him correctly.

"Here?" Thunder shook the old house. "Here?"

"Right here, thunder and all."

"It's a nice town but a bit noisy. Perhaps Beeder's Cove—"

"No. Thunder Ridge. I've got roots here."

"Roots?" She sputtered. "You call 'roots' a driving rain and folks stacked like cordwood in the icehouse? Roots?"

"Well." He eased closer. "I like things to be a little cluttered. Keeps life interesting."

She deflated. "You mean sort of like me cluttered."

"Sort of."

"I've changed."

A finger came up to tap her mouth. "Who said anything about change? I like you exactly the way you are."

She felt her gaze soften as he removed his hand. "I rather like you too."

"That's good. We like each other." He grinned. "Way ahead of where we were a few weeks ago."

"Yes, way ahead." Worlds ahead. The word *like* certainly did not describe even half of what she felt for him.

Audrey appeared in the doorway holding a breakfast tray. "Hey, you two. Breakfast is ready."

Josh stood up and moved out of the way as Audrey settled the steaming tray in front of Copper. She glanced at the bowl of oatmeal and lightly buttered toast and realized she couldn't eat a bite. His words had left her positively faint and hopelessly curious.

Redlin nodded to Audrey. "I was just on my way out. You take good care of this lady."

Audrey smiled. "Oh, I shall. She'll be good as new before very long."

He stood in the doorway turning the brim of his hat in his hands. Copper's eyes sought his. "You promise to write?"

"Twice a week."

"I'll answer three times a week."

He chuckled, turning faintly pink. "I'll not have an address that you can write to, but I'll think about you all week."

"Copper, you're embarrassing the man." Audrey adjusted

the tray and then turned and brushed past Josh on her way out. "Use your bell if you need anything."

"Thank you. I will."

Then there were just the two of them. He stepped back to the bed and bent to kiss her. She drank in his essence, the feel of his mouth touching hers, knowing it would be a long time, if ever, before they would be reunited.

When their lips parted, he whispered, "I will be back."

Nodding, she swiped at sudden hot tears rolling down her cheeks. So much could happen between now and then. So very much. She wasn't very old, but she'd lived long enough to be aware of the uncharted twists and turns life contained.

"Wait." She opened the small drawer in her bedside table and removed a pair of scissors. Snipping a lock of her hair, she put the token in an envelope, sealed it, and then slipped it into his shirt pocket. "So that you'll always remember me."

He chuckled. "I'll always remember you, Copper Wilson."

And then his mouth closed over hers and she forgot everything but him. Josh Redlin. Arrogant wagon master; honorable man of her dreams.

Please God, I'll never ask another thing if you'll bring him back to me.

The prayer was born of desire, and Copper knew God didn't always grant desires. Needs he promised to fulfill, but desires were optional.

Could she live without this man? Would her life still hold meaning and purpose without him to brighten her day?

Unfortunately she was about to find out.

He would be back. He said he would. Now she had to trust that he was the man she thought he was, a man of his word.

Chapter 21

C opper took the letter from Audrey and stuck it under the pillow.

"Hey—that's not fair." Her friend pulled up a chair. "Where is he? What does he say?"

Copper crossed her arms. "That's a private matter."

"Oh please. When has anything about your and Redlin's relationship ever been private?" She scooted the chair closer. "Come on. Open it."

"I will. The moment you leave." She was willing to share anything with her best friends, anything but Josh's correspondence. What if he had come to his senses sooner than she'd hoped and realized their attraction was completely unreasonable, and now that some distance separated them he planned to sever the tenuous bond? Distress so great it overcame her. No. He wouldn't do that. He was more principled than to give his word and go back on it.

But he'd never said that he was in love with her. His eyes, his glances, his touch left that impression, yet what man wouldn't try to console a woman with an injury as grave as hers had been? A horrifying thought struck her. That was why the letter had come so swiftly. He'd had time to reconsider the unlikely match and decided to end it swiftly and without further complication.

Sighing, Audrey pushed back. "Fine. Keep the letter to yourself."

"I intend to." Copper couldn't bear the thought of reading his rejection out loud to a woman whose one true love couldn't get enough of her.

"Are you aware that since that man left you've been on pins and needles? I declare I've never seen you so smitten."

"I'll get over it." If the letter contained what she thought it did, she had resolved to get over him quickly. Quickly—if a hundred years fit the criterion.

It was hard to believe that the old Copper could let such a disaster befall her. Until Redlin entered her life she'd done quite well without a man's companionship. But underlying her thoughts was the knowledge that she would never be the same Copper, the same naive, spoiled woman who first came to Thunder Ridge.

The bedroom door closed behind Audrey, and Copper drew the missive from under the sheet and ripped into it.

Copper,

It took five days for me to catch up with the train. Allison lost a wheel shortly after leaving the fort and the train was further delayed or it would have taken me longer.

Run-on sentence. She shook her head, grinning. Well, he'd never claimed to be a scholar.

> *I pray this letter finds you well and patient. By now you must be tired of being obedient and you're making life difficult for Audrey and Willow. Remember time is the key to your situation.*
>
> *I will write as often as I can find a post. We will be coming into rugged country before much longer so I'm not sure how often I can mail my letters but I will every chance that I get.*

Her grin widened. His English skills were deplorable; she had her work cut out for her.

> *You will never know how hard it was for me to ride away that morning. I pray that the injury will heal and the results will be no worse than a limp. We can live with that can't we?*
>
> Josh

She folded the letter and brought it to her chest, visualizing his arrogant grin. Her fears and determination to live without him were unnecessary. He had written that "we" could live with a limp. *We.* She savored the affirmation. Of course, if it was necessary, they could live with a limp. People lived with much worse, but that probably wouldn't be necessary. The injury was healing nicely according to Dr. Dyson. In another four weeks the bandage would come off, and her life would be the same as it was before the injury. She wouldn't embarrass Josh with her imperfection, though

Redlin didn't appear the type to allow superficial things to bother him. Yet she wanted to be perfect for him. Perfect in every way. A tap sounded at her door, and she slipped the letter beneath the sheets. "Yes?"

"Miss Wilson?"

She relaxed. No nosy friends wanting to know what the correspondence said. "Come in, Dr. Dyson."

The doctor entered, freshly shaved and looking and smelling considerably better than the first day they'd met. "How's my patient this morning?" He set a small bag on the bed, and Copper eyed it.

"You have a new satchel."

"Yes, thanks to Dr. Smith. He was gracious enough to provide me with a few instruments."

"He's a good man."

"That he is." His gaze centered on her bandaged ankle. "How is the pain level?"

"Better. I'm only taking something to help me sleep at night."

"Very good." He examined the foot, probing and then partially unwrapping the bandage and turning the injury to the window light. "Yes . . . the suturing is holding together well."

"What does that mean?"

Straightening, he smiled. "It means all looks well."

Hope sprang eternal. "Then you might have succeeded? It's still possible that I will walk without a limp?"

"Whoa. When I say 'well' I only mean coming along nicely. It will be weeks before we know the full results of my attempt." Pulling up a chair, he sat down. "Miss Wilson—"

"Please. Call me Copper. 'Miss Wilson' seems so formal

considering all that we're been through." After all, this man had become an important part of her life. "Miss Wilson" was entirely too proper.

He nodded. "Copper. As I was saying, though it will be weeks before we know with certainty about your ankle, I fear that at best, I have only scratched the surface of the injury."

She turned her head toward the window. "Please, allow me my hope." No one seemed willing to accept that a miracle might be in the making, though truthfully miracles didn't happen along that often.

"Of course, but I'm not God, nor do I understand his work. On the other hand, I cannot allow you to harbor false hope. Yours was the most serious injury of its type I've ever encountered in my long career, and I have no mystical powers."

"You underestimate your gift, Doctor. Your reputation is sterling and you're a reputedly exceptional surgeon."

"Perhaps, but sometimes a man's skills aren't enough." His features darkened. "Sometimes we're forced to accept the unacceptable."

"But what if you can't accept?" She didn't have his resilience, though goodness knew she'd seen that even a man like Dyson could fold when life dealt a major blow.

His gaze switched from the window and centered on her. "I wasn't aware we're given a choice."

A rap on the doorsill interrupted the conversation. Eli Gray's large frame filled the entrance. "Am I interrupting?"

"Eli, no. Come in." She motioned to the second chair. "You've met Dr. Dyson?"

"Briefly." The two men shook hands. "I trust you're settling comfortably at the widow's?"

"Very nicely. She cooks a mean pot roast."

Copper grinned at Eli. "Ah . . . the groom-to-be. You sly old fox. To what do I owe the pleasure?"

Color rose to his handsome features. "I stopped by to see Audrey. I'm about to take a load of lumber to Blackberry Hill and Audrey thought you might want me to stop by Betsy Pike's while I'm over that way."

"Oh yes, please. I need to pen a short note and let her know that I'm back." Judge Madison's former housekeeper was a dear friend. "Can you wait a moment?" She reached into her side table and took out a pen and paper.

Eli filled the ensuing void in the conversation as the doctor prepared to leave. "Understand you plan to return to the cavalry?"

"I haven't thought beyond my patient's recovery. Miss Wilson's recuperation will be complete in a few weeks."

"Well, I'm sure Doc Smith could use some help if you had a mind to settle somewhere. You from around these parts?"

"No. My wife and I came west twenty years ago when I joined up. We hail from Philadelphia."

Eli nodded. "So you have family there?"

"Very little. My mother is still living, and a distant cousin." He latched the bag. "Or they were last I heard."

"Thunder Ridge is noisy, but it's a friendly town," Eli noted. "We were nearly flooded out a few weeks ago, but the rain finally stopped."

"Too much of anything can be a bad thing," the doctor said.

Copper signed her name, shaking her head. Men. Their feelings ran as deep as women's, but they managed to contain their sentiments. She folded the note and stuck it in an envelope. "Please give Betsy my best."

"Thanks. I will." Eli stuck the letter in his shirt pocket, then reached to clasp the doctor's hand. Finally Copper recognized the inner light now shining in his eyes. "If I can be of help, you can find me at the mill."

"Thank you. Pleasure to make your acquaintance." The men shook. Copper didn't experience the pressure of the handshake but she'd guess Eli's was firm and encouraging.

When life was good, time flew past; when it wasn't, the hours crawled by like a wounded animal. If it weren't for Audrey and Eli's upcoming nuptials, Copper felt she would lose her mind. Being confined to a bed or a chair left long days to fill, hours when her heart and mind were with the wagon train slowly weaving its way to Colorado. Some of those days she was filled with hope; on others despair occupied her time. She'd grown accustomed to the monotony of travel, and while she didn't miss the bad roads and inclement weather, she did miss her friends. Sadie, Adele . . . and Josh. How she missed that man!

Sadie and Adele posted as often as possible. Their letters were full of wit, humor, and encouragement, but underlying the lightness, Copper knew the journey was more difficult than they'd anticipated. Winter had hit hard, and the dreary days and frequent cold rain slowed travel to a crawl.

Of late, Josh's letters contained little more than mention of the day's events, that for the most part consisted of stray stock and broken equipment. But the primary tone gave Copper hope.

"How can you help me with my wedding when all you do is stare out of the window?"

Audrey's teasing inflection drew her back to the present. Sighing, she picked up the gown Willow had worn when she exchanged vows with Tucker Gray. Was that only a few weeks ago? It seemed like eons. So much had happened since her first Thunder Ridge visit it made her head swim. So many life-altering events. She focused on Audrey's statement. "Don't you feel that it's too soon?"

"To marry Eli?" Audrey frowned. "Of course not. I've been in love with the man practically from the moment I saw him."

"No, silly. To wear the same gown Willow got married in."

"Oh." Audrey brought a finger to her lip. "I see your point."

Willow had been so ill at the time of her ceremony she'd mingled only a few minutes following the vow exchange, but the gown was so unusual that the sameness would be noted, especially by Cordelia Padget.

"You can ask Willow how she feels about the matter when she wakens from her nap."

"No, I'll not bring up the subject. You know Willow. She would insist that I wear the garment." Audrey folded the dress and laid it back in the box. "I don't need fancy dresses. I can wear my Sunday best. Marrying Eli is all I want."

Copper studied her friend's flushed features. Love changed people, softened their edges and tempered their dispositions. "You do love the man, don't you?"

"Eli? Beyond words." Audrey drew the box close to her heart. "Yet for so long I didn't let myself hope that he would come around and share my feelings so quickly."

"Well, love has a way of taking you by surprise."

Audrey turned to face her. "He asked me to wait for him

just before Willow and Tucker's ceremony. Of course I said yes, thinking it would take time for him to come around, to open up to a new relationship. But, goodness me, the man is moving so fast now it makes my head reel."

"He's ready for change. The healing process is different for everyone, and Tate does need a mother."

"You know, I love that child as much as if he were my own."

"He is your own, or he will be shortly."

"Speaking of change." Audrey met her gaze. "You've changed."

"How so?"

"You're quieter, less likely to spout off and . . . well, there's a bloom in your cheeks that wasn't evident earlier."

"A lot has happened in a short time."

"Josh?"

Copper nodded. "I love him, Audrey. I'd convinced myself he was the most arrogant man on earth before my accident, but he changed. Or I changed."

"Or you both changed."

"Yes, we've both changed, though I know next to nothing about his past. So I guess I can't make the assumption that he's different than before."

"He has mentioned little about himself." Audrey picked up her sewing. "But then men for the most part don't care to talk about such things."

"Oh, he's talked about his past, but offered few details. I know his father left the family when he was small, and he and his three brothers were left to run the farm and care for their mother."

"That's all he's said?"

"For the most part, but he writes regularly to a woman in Dallas."

Audrey frowned.

Copper lifted her shoulders. "I don't know who she is. I asked once and he almost took my head off."

"Really. Perhaps she's a sister? Oh—you said he only had brothers."

"And from the little I've gathered he doesn't keep in close touch with them."

"Mother?"

"Deceased now."

"Cousin? Aunt, perhaps?"

"Perhaps, but somehow I don't think he'd be so dedicated to write so often to an aunt. Every time we got a chance he dropped a letter in the mailbag."

"Strange. And yet he writes to you."

"Three letters now." Today had been the first week that she hadn't received his correspondence.

"Sounds like a smitten man to me."

"Yes." Copper sighed. "But with whom?"

"Oh, silly, with you. I don't know who this mysterious woman is that he writes to, but surely Josh isn't one to trifle with a woman's affections. There could be all kinds of reasons that he writes another woman. Why didn't you press him for an answer?"

"I couldn't. We haven't openly expressed our personal feelings. I would have been totally out of place."

"I would have pestered him until he told me."

"You're different than me."

"Not that different. If Eli were writing to another woman, that would be the first question on my lips."

"And he wouldn't have told you. You could barely get him to look your way not so long ago."

Grinning, Audrey rethreaded a needle. "But eventually I did, didn't I?"

"Granted."

"Nothing ventured, nothing gained."

"Clichés? Then I must say: You can lead a horse to water, but you cannot make him drink."

"Love and hate are two horns on the same goat."

"All's fair in love and war."

"Better to have loved and lost than never to have loved at all."

"Enough!" Copper surrendered. "I get the point."

"Good. So?"

"So what?"

"Are you going to ask him who this baffling woman is?"

"And how would I do that? I can't answer his letters because I don't have anywhere to send mail."

"He intends to come back to Thunder Ridge, doesn't he?"

Copper's thoughts skipped back to their last conversation. *I will be back, Copper.* "He said that he would."

Audrey looked up. "You doubt his word?"

"He's never given me any reason to distrust him."

"He'll be back."

Perhaps. Copper wanted to believe that he would, but so much could change in so short a period of time. She could personally testify to that.

"I wish I had your optimism."

"Admittedly, you have to work on confidence. When I was pursuing Eli I despaired more than once that he would never love anyone but Genevieve. But now he loves me. Willow thought she was destined to marry Silas Sterling, and instead the Lord sent her straight into Tucker Gray's arms. Now Silas has passed, and Willow, once she recuperates from this head injury, will have Tucker's babies, and the circle of life will go on."

Life had worked out so smoothly for Willow and Audrey. Copper had to believe that the good Lord had a surprise in store for her. When the bandage came off she would be able to walk across the floor even and steady. By the time Josh came back—and he would come back, she wouldn't permit herself to think otherwise—she would be whole again. They could pick up their relationship, and in a few months she might be looking for suitable wedding attire. She would teach school next year— or by then she and Josh might be ready to start a family.

Surprising how well this confidence thing worked.

"Oh, did I mention that we got another letter from Ester? She rambles on so! I gather she's getting senile. She's doing well in Kansas, though. If I weren't getting married I think I would make the trip there this summer and visit with her while she still has her mind."

Copper's thoughts skipped to the older woman from Timber Creek who had fought harder than any man. "She must be nearing fifty." Copper paused. "Aunt Nancy lives in Ellsworth, not far from where Ester settled. I must remember to write and tell her to seek Ester out. They would enjoy each other's friendship."

"Mmm. They are about the same age, aren't they?"

"No! Aunt Nancy is nearing seventy, to be certain. She's much older than Ester."

Resting her sewing in her lap, Audrey smiled. "Ellsworth. I hear it's a rowdy cattle town."

Audrey nodded. "They have a large rail stockyard there."

Leaning back, Copper closed her eyes. "Maybe when I get better I'll pay both Aunt Nancy and Ester a visit."

"Now what kind of talk is that? By then Josh will be back, and you'll be planning your own wedding."

"Perhaps."

Then again, Copper wasn't going to count chickens before they hatched. This was the first week she hadn't received Josh's letter. She'd be tempted to blame bad weather but Adele and Sadie had sent their posts. Weather had not kept Mike from the nearest post office.

But she wasn't going to let a week without letters from Josh dash her hopes.

What was a week other than seven long days?

Most likely Susan hadn't heard from him either.

Chapter 22

"Now Miss Wilson, I wouldn't read anything worrisome into this. That road to Colorado Springs is long and unpredictable. This time of year they could have run into anything." It was the fourth week Henry Martin had stood empty-handed in Copper's bedroom doorway. Even Sadie's and Adele's letters had stopped coming.

"It's been so long, Henry."

"I know, and the letters were coming as predictable as frost, but don't you be working yourself into a lather because you haven't heard from any of them for a while."

She bet Susan had heard from him.

Copper Wilson! You're turning as sour as a green apple. Thank the good Lord, the long weeks had passed and today the bandage came off and she could resume normalcy.

"Thank you, Henry. You've been so good to come over every week."

Henry turned to leave, then turned back. "Now I don't

want you fretting about Indians. That wagon train that was waylaid a while back couldn't have been Redlin's unless the weather forced him take a different route."

Copper slowly lifted her eyes. "A wagon train was attacked?"

"Shore—you've heard the . . ." He paused, eyes shifting uncomfortably.

"I've heard nothing. I live in this room."

"Oh. Well, nothing to break a sweat over. There was a small article in the *Post*. Just happened to notice it whilst I was delivering the paper to the judge's house. Probably nothing to it. You know how that sort of thing gets out of hand."

Nausea rose to the back of her throat. Willow and Audrey had withheld the paper from her. Josh? Was that why his letters had stopped coming?

No. They'd met with bad weather and had to hole up somewhere. He was fine. Just fine. Ornery as ever.

Dr. Dyson appeared in the doorway. "Good morning, Copper." He nodded to the postmaster. "Henry."

"Mornin', Doc!" Henry stepped out of the way. "Hear this is the big day."

Copper jerked back to the present. The bandage. In minutes now she would know her fate. That was all she'd been able to think about the past few days until now, until Henry mentioned that newspaper article.

"How old is the paper, Henry?"

"Beg pardon?"

"The paper with the article you mentioned."

He scratched his head. "Two—three weeks. But you cain't read nothing into that."

Oh, but she could. And she did. What else could account

for the sudden silence? The lack of letters? Certainly there was a multitude of possible reasons, but at the moment the most obvious and devastating one was all she could think of.

Audrey and Willow appeared, Willow winded from climbing three flights of stairs. Audrey sat her friend down in the bedside chair and then turned to Copper. "Well, this is the hour we've all been waiting and praying for."

"Where's the last *Post*?"

Willow glanced at Audrey. "Why . . . I'm not certain. Probably around here somewhere. Why do you ask?"

"I want to see it."

"Oh . . . I believe I threw the paper out when I was cleaning earlier this week," Audrey said. "I'm sorry. I thought you'd seen it."

Copper couldn't get Henry's dire words out of her mind. Had Josh been massacred? Was he now lying in an unmarked grave, dug by a passing stranger? Or not in a grave at all? A sudden chill swept her.

Dr. Dyson patted her hand. "The guessing will be over in a minute."

Copper could barely voice her turbulent thoughts. "I'm not concerned about the ankle . . . it's Josh. And Adele . . . Sadie."

"What about Josh?"

"Henry said there'd been another massacre."

Audrey caught her hand, eyeing Henry with a censuring look. "There was a small piece in the *Post*. It didn't identify the traveling parties and we didn't tell you because everyone feels certain that it couldn't have been Redlin's train. The route wouldn't have been one Redlin would have taken, not this time of the year."

Copper searched her friend's eyes looking for any sign of honest certainty. "Why are you so convinced? Worsening weather could have made him take a different direction. You know Josh; he does what he feels best for the travelers."

"The train would have been off course by at least twenty miles. You know Josh runs a tight ship."

"When he must. But he would be the first to change course if he felt the planned route posed danger."

"Still," Dr. Dyson interrupted, "let's not borrow trouble; today has enough of its own." He set his instrument bag on the bedside table. "Now then. Let's see if we can find some good news this morning."

A hush fell over the gathering as the doctor took a pair of small scissors and snipped the end of the bandage and then slowly unwound the cloth as the women and Henry looked on.

Copper closed both eyes. *God, a limp is nothing if only you have spared Josh's life.*

Bargaining with God? It was highly unlikely that he would negotiate, but she would fall to her knees and plead if it would help. She could, and would, accept anything if Redlin was beside her.

The bandage fell away and eyes fastened on the small ankle with a large angry scar running the length of the bone.

"In time the scar will lose its redness," the doctor said. "The incision looks clean and appears to be healing suitably."

Earlier his words would have produced euphoria but all Copper could think about was Josh. "The surgery was successful?"

"We'll know soon enough." He eased her to a sitting position. "I want you stand up."

"Stand up?"

"Put your weight on both ankles."

Goose bumps stood out on her arms. It had been so long since she'd walked, truly walked, unhampered by pain.

The doctor gently helped her off the mattress.

"Careful," Willow whispered.

"Don't overdo," Audrey echoed.

Copper's bare feet touched the icy floor. Suddenly prudence swept her. What if the injured ankle wouldn't hold her? What if she fell and hurt it a third time? Indecision flashed through her mind.

"It's okay," Dyson urged. "The ankle is tender. There'll still be some pain, but the bone is sufficiently on the mend."

Taking a deep breath, Copper straightened and took a cautionary movement. Smiles broke out as she took a tentative step. Then suddenly her knees buckled.

The doctor caught her before she collapsed to the floor. Grave-faced, he helped her back to the bed. The room was so silent Copper could hear her uneven breath.

Tucking the sheet around her, Dyson said, "I'm sorry. The bone will continue to knit and get stronger, but I'm afraid my efforts were largely in vain." His eyes met hers with compassion. "You will have a noticeable limp."

Catching her breath, she bit back bitter tears.

Bending close, he whispered. "What I'm about to say will bring little solace, but I've reminded numerous men, boys really, on the battlefield that they needed to rejoice over what they still had, little though it may seem, and always remember the old Persian proverb that goes something like: 'I met a man who cried because he had no shoes until one day he met a man who had no feet.' Life brings the cruelest disappointments and setbacks, yet for every gift taken away a new one is given."

Copper dabbed at the moisture running down her cheeks and then reached for his hand. "Do you honestly believe that, Doctor? Not so long ago I heard you railing against God about life's injustices. You demanded that we didn't speak of God in your presence. So I ask you again; do you really believe that there is a God-given purpose for every bad thing that happens in life?"

"A purpose, you ask." His hold on her hand tightened. "If man has no function, life would be quite a meaningless farce, wouldn't it? I have yet to meet a mortal that could ever design all the intricate details of life. I fear that I often rail at God, but because of his grace he has seen fit to ignore my complaints. As to purpose, well, isn't that what life is? Humanity filling a purpose, both good and bad?"

Dabbing her nose, Copper whispered. "I'd trade knowing where Josh is, and if he's safe, for walking a mile on both feet."

Squeezing her hand, the doctor rose. "I'm going to rebind the foot, but you're free to move about. Be very careful with that ankle for another month, and let the bones finish mending."

Wordlessly, Copper sank back to the pillow.

Over the next month, short outings turned into brief walks, which evolved into longer excursions. In addition to self-indulgence, guilt started to creep into her thoughts. Audrey claimed that Eli could not spare sufficient time away from the mill, but Copper knew the couple delayed their wedding nuptials because of her. Audrey's distress shown in her eyes, and Copper knew she'd never leave her in her time of need. Perhaps she encouraged Audrey's unfathomable loyalty; at this point she wasn't certain of anything but days of unending despair. She was literally awash in despondency, a state she both welcomed and despised.

The day arrived when Copper felt physically strong enough to tackle a full day's outing. Dressed warmly against a chilling wind, she held to Audrey's and Willow's protective arms. When alone, she needed a crutch, but she could do without it when she had a shoulder to lean on. Not a word had been sent by Josh, Adele, or Sadie. The only logical conclusion was one she couldn't bring herself to accept. But reality forced her to admit that Josh and her friends might be gone.

Shrugging free from the coddling, she straightened. "I can walk now, thank you."

"We don't want you to fall and hurt yourself," Willow rebuked.

"Then I should hold *your* arm because you're still weak as a kitten."

"Not as a kitten," Willow denounced. "Maybe a sizable tomcat, but not a helpless kitten."

Copper hobbled on, determined for the first time to walk unaided. Days meant nothing. Outings meant nothing. Her life meant nothing. Why did God keep her around? She had no purpose or meaning, regardless of Dr. Dyson's theories. Josh was dead. Though she wouldn't permit herself to voice the thought, she knew.

She knew.

"Copper, it breaks my heart to see you so despondent." Audrey sidestepped a pile of snow. "I know life hasn't been easy for you of late, but you mustn't lose hope."

Copper turned to note Audrey's nice, easy gait. "Easy for some to say."

Shaking her head, Audrey walked on. "You're hopelessly cranky. Why don't I have Tucker hitch up the buggy and we take a ride to Beeder's Cove? You can visit with the children. I know they must be concerned about your welfare, and you do need to pay Emily and Mackey's grandfather your respects and personally thank him for the excellent care he's provided you."

"To no avail."

"Please." Audrey paused. "I won't claim that I know how you feel. I don't make light of the surgery's disappointing outcome or the sudden lack of correspondence from Josh. But you must pull out of this depression. You're a young woman with your future ahead of you. You mustn't sit down and wither away like a grape in the fall."

Copper fixed her eyes on the path. "And what would you have me to do, Audrey? Rejoice that I walk like an ogre, that I've lost the only man on earth that . . ." Her voice cracked with emotion. She regained control. Bitterness engulfed her. "Perhaps I will purchase an imitation hand that looks like a pirate's hook and terrify the children in Thunder Ridge."

"Now, now," Willow scolded. "Enough dramatics. There are so many possible reasons why you haven't heard from Josh or Adele and Sadie, reasons too numerous to count. Let's not think the worst until we have certain reason to fear."

"You know very well there's reason to 'fear.'"

"Yes, I won't deny that my thoughts run much in the same vein as yours, but we don't know for sure." She paused and turned Copper to face her. "We *don't* know. If Josh were standing here he'd admonish you to have faith even though it is the size of a mustard seed."

"Doesn't work. I 'had faith.' I *prayed* long and hard that the surgery would be successful, and you see how that's turned out."

The women fell silent as they continued through the cold. Finally Willow ventured, "Oh, there's Tucker. I think a visit to Beeder's Cove is just what we need."

Shrugging, Copper paused. Where they went, or what they did, was inconsequential to her.

Tucker readily agreed to Willow's plan and shortly brought around a surrey hitched to a high-stepping mare. The women climbed aboard and wrapped themselves in warm blankets.

Tucker personally checked Willow's comfort and stole a long kiss before he handed her the reins. So lengthy that Copper looked away, the ache in her heart so deep she thought she'd welcome death.

Audrey's gaze wandered to the office, and seconds later Eli emerged. Bending close, he kissed her. "I hear you're going to Beeder's Cove?"

"Yes. Will you miss me?"

His gaze softened to one of a man completely smitten. "I'll tell you how much tonight at supper."

Copper turned away. Oh how she despised her apathy. She was awash in overemotional self-pity. Somewhere in her unsettled mind she knew her emotional condition but was powerless to emerge from the storm. Not so long ago she would have had little patience for someone like her. Now she felt nothing.

With a flick of her wrists Willow started the horse toward Beeder's Cove. Copper tried to focus on anything but the affectionate exchanges. She'd been mistaken. She did care where she went today. Why had she ever agreed to this inane trip?

Approaching hoofbeats caught her attention and she turned to see a rider coming up fast. Recognizing the rider she called, "Willow! Stop!"

The horse slowed and Willow turned to look back. "What's wrong?"

"Henry Martin is trying to catch us." The women waited until the man caught up.

When he rode alongside he was grinning ear to ear. "Thank goodness I finally caught your attention."

"What's wrong?"

He waved a letter in Copper's face. "This just came!"

Her heart shot to her throat. She snatched the envelope, her eye going to the return address. *Adele.*

"Is it from Josh?" Copper asked.

"No. Adele." She ripped into the letter and began to read.

Hi Honey,

I know you must be worried sick about us, but we've just had one problem after the other. We had eight rigs mired in mud a good two weeks. Like to never got them out and rolling again, but we finally got on the road but then it was one thing after the other and we just plain made bad time. But we're finally here, safely in Colorado Springs and the sights are the likes of which you've never seen. Mountains so tall they take your breath, and the air is clean though it's a bit hard to breathe up here. We're getting used to it.

Most have already set out to stake their claims, but me and Sadie decided to stay put for a while. Don't know exactly where we'll end up, but I'll write when we find a place where we want to live.

Josh took off for Dallas practically the minute we rolled into town. Said he had business, but I feel like we didn't have decent enough time to say good-bye.

I'm sure by now you're bouncing all over the place with two good ankles. Feels real good, doesn't it? The trip was a long one, but meeting up with Dr. Dyson was a real blessing.

I'll write more later.

Your good friend, Adele

P.S. Sadie says howdy. Soon as she gets the money for a stamp she will write too.

Josh took off for Dallas practically the minute we rolled into town. The words stood out on the page as though they were made of fire.

"What does it say? How come they haven't written? Is Josh okay?"

Wadding the letter into a tight ball, Copper threw it aside. "They're there. Everyone's fine. Josh took off for Dallas almost the moment they got there."

A hush fell over the group. Finally Henry spoke. "Well, guess that means he'll be coming back real soon."

Copper turned away. "Don't get your hopes up."

The surrey rolled into Beeder's Cove around the noon hour. The children were playing behind the small house that had been turned into a temporary school, dressed in coats and mittens, kicking a ball around the yard.

Helping Copper out of the buggy, Willow smiled. "Does your heart good, doesn't it, to see all these young children at play." She sighed. "How I miss the schoolroom."

"I share your feelings. Now that everything is back to normal, I plan to start Thunder Ridge classes next week," Audrey said. She turned to Willow. "Are you sure you won't change your mind and decide to step back into the position? The job is really yours, and I'm certain I can secure work in Blackberry Hill, if need be."

Willow's clear laugh rang out. "I am most certain. Tucker wants children just as soon as I gain enough strength to be a mother. I can hardly teach and take care of a new baby at the same time."

"Well." Audrey worried her lower lip. "Eli would like children soon once we marry." The women turned to focus on Copper.

She shook her head. "I told you. I don't have any plans."

"But you must," Audrey accused. "You can't just shrivel up and die. Josh will come back, and if he doesn't . . ." She glanced at Willow. "The Lord has something or *someone* better in store for you." Audrey's tone held the first hint of disapproval.

"Please. This was supposed to be a heartening outing." Copper limped ahead of her friends and maneuvered the two wooden steps leading into the temporary schoolhouse. A young woman turned her head as the front door opened and Copper entered, trailed by Willow and Audrey.

Laying an apple aside, Carrie Wyman sat at the desk, smiling. "May I help you?"

Introductions followed and the teacher seemed delighted to finally meet the "wonderful Miss Wilson" that the children had been asking about so often.

Copper's eyes roamed the room. The last time she'd been here the building had been an empty house. "I suppose they'll rebuild the schoolhouse?"

Carrie turned to trace her gaze. "Yes, I believe they plan to start work this summer." She turned back to face Copper. "You are as lovely as the children said you were. I trust your injury is healing properly?"

"Thank you. The ankle is healing." Moving past the new teacher, Copper stepped over to read the writing on the chalkboard, leaving Audrey and Willow to explain. She'd told the story so many times she couldn't bear to repeat it. She was crippled. End of subject.

The women spoke in hushed, benevolent tones and Copper blocked out their voices. Her eyes skimmed the arithmetic problems written in chalk. One child thought 4 + 1 made 6. Carrie Wyman looked young, maybe sixteen, seventeen. She was fresh and bubbly, everything Copper wasn't. At the moment Copper felt as old as Asa Jeeters, who'd helped fight off the Yankees in Timber Creek. To his credit, Asa had gone down fighting; Copper had gone down like a wounded hummingbird.

Carrie checked her timepiece, excused herself, and stepped outside to ring the bell. Children poured into the schoolhouse. When Mackey and Emily spotted Copper, the two former pupils rushed into her arms.

She held the small, cold bodies close, drinking in the scent of fresh air and the unique smell of little boys and girls.

"We miss you, Miss Wilson." Mackey stood back, grinning.

"Look!" He displayed a mouth with a multitude of missing teeth.

"You've lost your front teeth, Mackey!"

"Yes, ma'am. And this one"—he bent closer—"and this one and this one."

"My goodness. Aren't you the fortunate one?"

"Yes, ma'am." The child beamed. "Only it's going to be real tough eating corn on the cob if they don't come back in."

Others gathered around and Copper caught up on their lives since the fire. Every child wanted a personal look at the injured ankle, and Copper obediently held her right boot up for inspection. "There's nothing to see with my boot on, only a little swelling."

"Oh." Little Stella frowned. "Does it hurt?"

"Not anymore." Copper smiled. "I'll be just fine, Stella. Are you keeping up on your reading?"

"Uh-huh." The child grinned. "I've read three books since school started."

"Very good. I'm proud of you." She patted the child and then impulsively drew her close for a protective hug. If only she could shield these children from life's uncertainties. Copper realized what she must do. She missed this part of her life, missed it so badly. She must leave for a while, gain a new perspective about her life. Perhaps the thought had been buried in her mind before this moment, but now it was clear. Somehow holding Stella helped her focus through all the anger, confusion, and disappointment that had been rolling around in her mind. From somewhere came a resolve she didn't know she had. No matter how much she'd like to bury her head in the sand, she knew she couldn't do it. She still had feelings. She didn't necessarily want them or like them, but nature had a way of overcoming reluctance, and as much as she denied it, she still loved teaching. Still ached with disappointment over Josh and her injury, but still reveled in the warmth of a child's embrace. Perhaps her life wasn't over; altered to be certain, different from her expectations, but not over. In time she could make a new life. While Audrey and Willow had babies and kept houses for their doting husbands, she could be the best "auntie" in the whole world.

Rising, she released Stella. "May I have a brief word with you, Miss Wyman?"

"Certainly." Carrie turned to address the class. "I shall allow talking, but no hitting or shouting."

Stepping outside and pulling the door closed behind her, the young schoolteacher wrapped her shawl tighter against a north wind. "You wished to speak to me?"

"Yes." Copper glanced at Willow and Audrey. "May we have a word in private?"

"Oh . . . of course." Audrey drew Willow off the step and they walked to the waiting surrey.

"She's so horribly down," Audrey murmured. "Don't you think we should tell her that Josh was the man who bought Judge Madison's home?"

"Goodness no!" Willow exclaimed. "He made us promise not to breathe a word, and what if this woman in Dallas is a suitor? Perhaps he bought the home for her."

"I can't bear to see her this way. So hateful. So despondent. That isn't Copper. She was always strong, relied on herself but never forgot the Lord was her source of strength."

"I know, and I have tried everything to pull her out of this phase but nothing works. If Josh doesn't come back . . ."

"If he's alive he will come back."

"But if this mysterious Susan means more to him than Copper does—"

"She doesn't. We can't permit ourselves to think anything but honorable thoughts of Josh Redlin, regardless of our limited knowledge. We know that he plans to settle in Thunder Ridge or he wouldn't have purchased the judge's home. We promised to keep his secret."

"What if he's bought the house for Susan?"

"Oh my." Audrey shook her head. "How much more can she bear?"

"Not a word, Audrey."

"All right. I won't say a word, but I hate keeping this from her."

"So do I, but we gave our word."

Copper watched as the women got into the carriage before she spoke. "Carrie—may I call you Carrie?"

"Please do."

"You seem very settled, even content here."

A smile broke across her youthful features. "Oh yes. I've always wanted to teach. I love children."

"And it shows." Copper forced a smile. "I'm considering visiting my aunt in Kansas and I was wondering if you would be willing to accept the teaching position on a permanent basis?"

A soft gasp escaped the schoolmarm and her face lit up with excitement. "Oh, Miss Wilson, I would love it, but . . ."

"No buts." This time Copper didn't have to force a smile. "I'm going to leave the area shortly, and I don't plan to return for a while. I'd like to keep my options open." She reached out and touched the young woman's arm, a young woman who had so much ahead of her. "The children seem very content. You're doing a marvelous job. I know I'm leaving my students in capable hands."

"Thank you." Carrie returned the affectionate gesture. "And I will pray that you find true happiness. You've surely given me a great gift."

"I'll submit my resignation to Mr. Fowler before I leave today. I'm sure he'll be delighted to keep you on."

"Again, thank you." The new teacher's eyes sparkled with gratitude. And why not? She was young, healthy, and given the gift to shape young minds. In time Copper would teach again, but not now. Right now all she wanted or needed was a fresh start, to find meaning for her life. The only absolute at the moment was the need to flee, to seek sanctuary from an existence that confused her.

And she was not going to breathe a word of her plans to either Audrey or Willow until she was ready to leave. She would inform Benjamin Fowler of her resignation, pay an obligatory visit to Mackey and Emily's grandfather, and then pay Aunt Nancy and Ester, in Kansas, a long overdue visit. Who knew? Maybe she'd take to Nancy's Ellsworth, the rough-and-tumble cattle town, and just stay there.

Chapter 23

⁓

Copper's hands jerked when a gun went off just outside.
She had moved close to the window so she could have
better light for her sewing, but it made the noises from outside even more distracting. She was getting used to the sound
of gunfire, but this one was much closer than most. She set
her jaw and stitched the last of the lace trim.

She glanced up at Aunt Nancy, a sparrowlike woman with
thick snow-white hair braided and secured tightly on the top
of her head by a hair pick. Ageless, the spirited bundle tot-
tered on a ladder to dust a top shelf. Copper eyed the teeter-
ing stance and sucked in a breath. It was useless to scold; Aunt
Nancy went where she pleased and did what she wanted.
Any mention to her of "Be careful" or "Aren't you a little too
old to be . . ." got you a look that plainly said, "No, I'm not"
and suggested that you not broach the subject again.

She glanced out the window that read *Glessner's Alterations*, but paid scant attention to three young cowboys spur-

ring their horses to a dead run side-by-side down the dusty street. More gunshots rang out.

Cackling, Aunt Nancy dusted away. "Ain't this 'bout the most excitin' town you've ever been in?"

Exciting? For sure. But Copper's opinion of the place didn't include the admiration that Aunt Nancy felt. Copper thanked God for her life when she safely reached her room each night.

Ellsworth, Kansas, offered haven to notorious gunmen, bull whackers, soldiers, army scouts, buffalo hunters, not to mention Cheyenne and, sometimes, pro-slavery raiders. Copper soon learned that the community had a reputation for being a violent place.

Climbing down off the ladder, Nancy stood back to survey her work. Outside the window two young cowhands were wrestling on the board sidewalk. People walking by simply went around them, paying them little heed.

Copper shook her head in disgust. "Seems a little loud today, don't you think, considering it's only Monday?"

Auntie's eyes sparkled. "Don't you just love a little excitement?"

"I've enjoyed all the excitement I can stand, thank you." Copper finished the row of lace, and her left foot paused on the treadle. "You seem to actually enjoy this violence." She still had not been able to get accustomed to the shootings, fistfights, and nightly brawls in front of the scandalous saloons where wanton women beckoned men inside.

"Honey, you know Mondays don't hold a candle to Saturday nights. A little fight now and again is a Sunday school meeting compared to Saturday night." Nancy hooted. "That's when this town gets exciting. When those cowpokes hit town with a month's pay, have a bath and a fifty-cent steak, why, that's when the fun begins. Once those boys get liquored up there's no tellin' what they'll do." She flicked a speck of dust off a lampshade. "That's what I call excitement."

Shaking the dress free of wrinkles, Copper wondered why she ever thought she could find respite here. Ellsworth was nothing like she'd anticipated. She'd yet to find anything to endear her to the raucous atmosphere. There was nothing attractive in the stench of cattle pens, the dust that turned to mud with the slightest shower, the sight of men sleeping off a drink in the alleys and loud piano playing coming from the saloons. The town was nothing like Thunder Ridge or Beeder's Cove.

There wasn't a moment when memories of Josh didn't weigh on her mind. She was sure that at this moment he was living happily in Dallas with Susan and she'd wager he never gave her a thought. Or did he?

She shook the notion away. He didn't want her. And why would he? The limp was worse than she feared, she was alone and lonely, and she had precious few prospects beyond being in a strange town with this strange little woman. Nancy was her mother's sister, and they were nothing at all alike. While her mother had been fiery and spirited, Nancy was a loose cannon, going off at the most unnerving times. She had always been a bit quaint, but it hadn't taken Copper long to discover that her beloved auntie was the town loon. When Copper arrived, Nancy had latched on to her, and there wasn't a spare moment that she didn't have the wiry woman by her side. The first night she had settled into a fitful slumber. When she stretched her toes in search of the warm hot water bottle, her feet touched another foot. Aunt Nancy had crawled in the bed beside her. When she'd asked why, the old woman said she hated to sleep alone, that Copper was a gift from God. She never intended to sleep alone again.

Every night Copper teetered on a thin sliver of mattress, keeping to her side. But before the night was over the woman who smelled of musk and liniment would crowd her to the point that she'd be forced to sleep in the chair, where she would remain most of the night.

Her heart ached. She missed Audrey and Willow. She'd been a fool to leave Thunder Ridge. She'd only replaced thunder with gunshots, and her depression was as deep and dark as ever. She'd locatd her friend Ester, who had fought battles with her. She'd found her some ten miles from Ellsworth, then discovered the woman had completely lost her mind. She couldn't remember the time of day, so their visits were short and pointless. She recalled last Sunday's visit while sitting on Ester's front porch.

"Lovely day, isn't it, Ester?"

The woman turned tolerant eyes on her. "Have we met?"

Copper repeated the same information she'd given each visit. "Yes, we fought together in Timber Creek. My name is Copper Wilson."

"Oh." Ester rocked, and then she turned to look at her. "Who'd I fight?"

"The Yankees . . . remember. You, me, Willow, Audrey, Asa Jeeters . . ."

"The town drunk?"

"Yes, you remember Asa."

She pulled her shawl closer. "Of course I remember Asa. Do you think I'm senile?"

"Not at all."

After a moment she looked back. "Have we met?"

Copper's life consisted of her new job at Mr. Glessner's

establishment, sewing alterations and ladies' gowns, and wallowing in a chair at night. It probably didn't matter if she was in the bed or not, since Nancy's snoring was usually loud enough to rattle china. She failed to see how she'd helped herself. She ought to go to Dallas, find Josh Redlin, and give him a piece of her mind. She glanced up, frowning.

"Aunt Nancy, please don't eat paste."

The woman looked up, her fingertip buried in a jar. "I like the taste."

"Doesn't matter. The vile habit is going to make you sick."

"Hasn't yet, and I've been eating it for years." She took a lick. "Doctor said I was going to die if I didn't quit snuff."

"So you've taken to eating paste?"

She nodded, extending the jar. "Have a bite."

"I don't want a bite."

She moved closer and shoved the jar beneath Copper's nose. "Come on, you'll like it. What's folks got against paste?"

Copper pushed the container aside. "I don't want any."

"Well." Nancy took a final swipe. "Suit yourself, but you don't know what you're missing." She smacked her lips, looking thoughtful now. "You know your problem, darling. You're like your mother. You try to run your life and forget there's a higher source in charge."

Copper pushed the treadle, hemming a skirt now, trying to ignore her. Where had that come from? Aunt Nancy didn't know her "problems." She hadn't mentioned a word about Josh Redlin or how desperately she missed him.

"Yep." Nancy wiped paste off her finger. "Just like your mother." She replaced the lid. "If you don't need me, guess I'll go on down to Suttler's Store and see what's going on. Usually one good shootin' a day down there."

"That's fine, Aunt Nancy." Copper slipped the dress on a hanger. Mr. Glessner was kind enough to let Nancy hang around, but Copper knew she made him nervous. When she appeared, he disappeared to the back room and worked on men's tailoring. "I'll be home a little after five."

Home? For her, neither Ellsworth nor the small room in Aunt Nancy's house qualified as a home. Truth was, she longed for Thunder Ridge where weather was the only real threat to one's sanity. Changing a spool of thread, she wondered why she had stayed this long. Six weeks wasn't an eternity, and yet today it felt like it. She drew a deep breath and admitted to herself that she still hoped the visit would erase memories. It hadn't yet, and she was losing hope that she would ever eradicate Josh Redlin's time in her life. Yes, he was a cad of the worst sort, and he had misled her into thinking that he would be back. Yet her feelings for him hadn't changed. She loved the lout, imperfect as he might be. She must learn to face life without him.

Aunt Nancy started out the door when Copper suddenly called, "Auntie?"

The woman turned. "Eh?"

"Am I really like Mother?" Copper had never thought of the comparison, but Mother, though a dear, was stubborn, loving. Kind. She was everything Copper thought herself to be.

"Honey." Aunt Nancy pulled up a chair and sat down. "You're the spittin' image of Luanna, God love her. Oh, she was a pistol, that one. Good as they come, but you get her dander up and you had yourself a peck of trouble. Now your daddy knew how to deal with her. I always said the good Lord picked the one man with the patience of Job to marry Luanna. She had a heart of gold; do just about anything anyone ask of her but behave."

Copper bit back a grin. Funny how she'd forgotten Mama's temperament. Her "stubborn streaks," Father would say. Sometimes the household was in turmoil as Mama flew through the house like fury. She had the faith of a stewing hen, yet she loved the Lord and wouldn't stand for heathenish talk. She'd speak of trust and yet she rarely practiced it. Always fretted about nothing, stewed until she made herself sick with worry.

And yet she was Mother, and Papa and Copper loved the woman to pieces.

"You know, honey." Aunt Nancy leaned in closer. "I may appear a bit strange but I'm smarter than you think. Your mother got Pa's nature; I got my ma's common sense. There's not much in this old life that you can't overcome, with the help of our Maker. And that man you're pining away for—"

"I never said I was pining . . ."

Nancy held up a restraining hand. "You didn't have to say a word. It's written all over you, and what woman hasn't loved a man and feared that she'd lose him."

Defense crumbling, Copper buried her face in her hands. "But I have lost him, Aunt Nancy."

"That's a fact?"

"As close as I can tell."

"Close? But not a fact. Yet." The old woman reached out and put her hand on Copper's heaving shoulders. "Until it's a square hit, you haven't got a fact. You got a theory. And theories are known to be proven wrong."

Good heavens. Aunt Nancy knew the word *theory* and used it properly? What was this world coming to?

"Well, got to be going. They've probably already shot someone down at Suttler's and I've missed it."

The door closed behind her, and Copper settled back in her chair.

Outside, two men shouted and cursed at each other, and she recognized the buildup to another fight. This time, for some reason, a crowd was gathering to watch. This was the final straw. She swallowed hard to control the nausea that rose up in her stomach. She had to get out of this place. She had to go home. Beeder's Cove. Thunder Ridge. It didn't matter; she had to leave this insanity.

"Better the devils I know back there than the ones waiting around every corner here in Ellsworth," she said aloud.

Theory. Maybe Aunt Nancy was wiser than she thought.

The stage rolled into Thunder Ridge toward evening. It had taken a pretty penny to convince the driver to detour the few miles in order to drop her off, but she'd made a pretty penny over the past few weeks so she could afford the luxury.

She stepped from the coach beneath a leaden sky. Tom was sweeping the mercantile porch as she paid the driver and added a handsome tip. The stage rolled away and she turned and picked up her two bags. *Home.* Now Audrey and Eli would surely marry. The feeling seeped through her bones like the familiarity of one's own bed.

Nodding to the curious mercantile owner, she walked toward the ugly green house that towered above the smaller buildings, only . . . Her steps faltered. The house was no longer green. It was white, with pretty brown shutters and a new porch, a very large porch encircling the now striking exterior.

"I'd like to know how you accomplished that."

She turned to see that Tom had followed her. "Pardon?"

He scratched his head. "How in the cat hair did you get a stage line to bring you here?"

"Oh, that." She sighed. "Tom, I've discovered that given enough money you can get anyone to do almost anything." She turned back to stare at the house. "I see much has changed in the brief time I've been gone." Tucker managed money well, but she hardly thought he could scrape together enough to accomplish this amazing transformation.

"Oh yes, the house." The mercantile owner crossed his arms and stared at the renovation. "Downright attractive, isn't it."

"Tucker did this?"

"Tucker? He wouldn't have the money to do this. The new owner did it."

"Oh yes, the new owner. Then he must be planning to live here soon."

"Yep, that's what he claims. He, his wife, and their young'uns."

"He has children?" Her thoughts shifted to the school. Audrey would have additional pupils.

"Not yet." Tom walked off, wiping his hands on his apron.

Picking up her bags, Copper continued to the newly renovated house, picturing the surprise that awaited Audrey and Willow. Their last letter had been brimming with excitement about the upcoming wedding. The sawmill was running smoothly now, and Eli could take the time to enjoy a honeymoon. The wedding was set for the end of the month, and Copper was expected to be in attendance. The black shroud that had been covering her finally started to lift. She was deeply ashamed of her lack of faith. Nothing had changed other than the fact she knew she had succumbed to her fears and allowed them to dominate her. Biting her lower lip, she willed back tears. If she was going to live in Thunder Ridge she would have to shake this melancholy and truly celebrate Eli and Audrey's love. No one deserved happiness more than those two.

Breathless, she paused before the house, still stunned by the transformation. Cordelia Padget must be frantic. She'd wanted this house so badly. Willow had said the poor woman had taken to bed for a week when she was outbid at the auction. Suddenly the thought struck her. Had the new owner moved in? If so, where were Tucker and Willow staying? And Audrey?

Her eyes traveled to the sawmill site, seeking a familiar face.

"Well as I live and breathe. If it isn't Miss Wilson."

Whirling, Copper came face to face with Josh. For a second the air left her lungs and her throat closed. He was here! He'd really come back! Her eyes devoured him like a hungry child looking at a candy counter.

Then anger flooded her. He was *here*. Not in Dallas. Here in Thunder Ridge. Her pulse raced. He had come back—and she had left.

"I . . ." She searched but words failed her. She couldn't take her eyes off him, clean shaven, wearing buckskin trousers and a white shirt. She drank in the sight of red wavy hair, strong jawline. She swallowed, summoning self-righteous anger. Why should she be on the defensive? He'd chosen to go to Dallas before coming back to her.

"Speechless?" He quirked a brow. "That's not like you."

Her chin lifted with defiance. "You don't know me."

He shifted stances, a sure sign she was stepping on his nerves. "I'm about to think you're right. What is it about 'I'll be back' that you don't understand?"

Dropping both bags to the ground, she met his eyes. "How was Dallas?"

Chapter 24

"Hot. How was Ellsworth?"

"Scared the living daylights out of me." Her eyes narrowed. So he knew where she'd been, and he hadn't come after her. She stepped up on the porch. She was going to look him straight in the eye and demand to know why he had led her to believe they might have a future together.

He shifted. "So we've established that Dallas was hot and Ellsworth scared the living daylights out of you."

Shrugging, she looked away. Suddenly her accusations stuck in her throat. Truth was, he'd come back and she'd left. Silence followed the exchange until her nerves stretched thin.

"Where are Tucker and Willow?"

"Tucker's at the mill, and I would imagine Willow's with Audrey. Those two have been tight as ticks planning the wedding."

Jealously mixed with resentment. She should have been

here helping them plan. Instead she'd been in Kansas sleeping next to a strange, paste-eating, but oh-so-wise aunt and trying to forget the man standing in front of her existed. She spied the bucket of paint in his hand as he stepped around her. "What are you doing?"

"Painting."

"Painting what?"

"If you must know, painting my house."

"*Your* house." She turned to look at the renovation again.

He nodded, touching the brush to a corner. "That's what I said."

Her heart sank deeper than a rock in a well. *His house.* He had purchased the house, and he and Susan would be living here? With children. He had children! Bile swelled to the back of her throat. He'd deliberately misled her, told her he wasn't married. She couldn't bear it; she couldn't bear seeing him with another woman day after day, year after year. She couldn't endure him seeing her hobbling around the town like a pitied spinster. She closed her eyes, taking in drafts of air. But she couldn't, she simply refused to go back to Ellsworth. "You're planning to live here?"

He stepped down and propped his ladder against the steps, then hung his bucket of paint on a piece of wire hooked around a rung. Her thoughts churned. Audrey and Willow. They must have known that he'd purchased the house, known it all along, and not said a word to her. What had they hoped? That she would go away, as she had, and stay away? That she would never know that Josh was married to his mysterious lady in Dallas and he actually planned to move here? Raise their children here. Oh, she wanted to strike out, hurt him as much as she was hurting right now. This was the cruelest thing anyone had ever done to her. And she couldn't believe her best friends had betrayed her.

Whirling to leave, she discovered her flight blocked by the ladder.

"Move this thing!"

He started to comply but her anger burst. She shoved the contraption aside but it twisted and tipped. She saw the paint begin to spill and reached out to catch it. Instead she only managed to make it lean worse and splash on her face and down the front of her dress. Josh jumped clear, then back to help her. Their eyes locked and Redlin froze.

Drawing a deep breath, she made a few ineffective efforts to brush off the dripping liquid. Then she spun on her heel and started to descend the steps. She could feel his eyes on her back, on the limp. Tears blurred her vision. Confusion overwhelmed her. She felt . . . sensed that he had feelings for her. Deep feelings. She'd seen it in his eyes the brief instant their eyes had met. How could he be married to Susan and still have feelings for her? She stumbled and suddenly he was there, lifting her into his arms. She buried her face in his shoulder—the sweet, sweet scent of him—and allowed him to carry her to the side of the house where a can of turpentine and cloth awaited. Gently he began to clean the paint off her face.

"You are one hard-to-figure-out woman, Miss Wilson."

"Why did you lie to me?"

"I didn't lie to you. I told you I would be back. Why didn't you wait for me?"

Why indeed. That would be the question that she would take to her grave, but he couldn't know how devastated she had been when she was first convinced there was another woman. He had a right to happiness, and if he and Susan . . . She couldn't bear the thought of him and Susan.

"You left for Dallas the moment you reached Colorado. Why didn't you at least write and tell me you were married."

He held her at arm's length. "Who said I was married?"

"Adele wrote and told me," she said.

"That I was married?"

"No. That you left for Dallas the moment you got to Colorado. Or shortly afterwards, I'd assume."

"I told her to write and tell you."

"Is this a continuation of your game, Mr. Redlin? Have Adele tell me that you were off to see Susan, prepare me for the time you would bring her here?" She caught her breath on a sob. "Well, I don't blame you. She's probably perfect, and I'm not. Two perfect people. With how many children? Two? Three? How could you!" She jerked aside and limped away.

"Children!"

"How many, Mr. Redlin? Five, six?"

He caught up with her and led her back to the turpentine. "You just hold on, young lady. Adele doesn't know my relationship with Susan." He lifted the rag and started to scrub her face.

"Ouch . . . you're hurting me. And she *does* know. I told her and the other women that you were writing to a woman in Dallas named Susan."

"But neither Adele nor the other women knew why, and neither did you. Six kids? I don't have one child. That's why I warned you against spreading tales you knew nothing about.

You're lucky I don't turn you over my knee like a willful child and whup you."

"You and whose army?"

He scrubbed paint out of her hair. "For the life of me, I can't understand your fixation on Susan."

"You can't understand that I would be concerned that the man I love might be in love with another woman? A woman he wrote regularly, married evidently, a woman he went directly to when the journey ended." She caught back a sob. "You don't need to answer. Susan is a whole woman, not a cripple like me. But you couldn't have known I was a cripple, Josh. You didn't bother to ask the results of my—" She wiped back tears. "And you've made me a disgraced woman, a woman who fell in love with a married man."

He grasped her shoulders firmly. "Stop right there."

She resisted. "Let me go!"

He pinned her to his side, holding her tightly until the fight went out of her. "Yes I went to Susan first. Now you've heard me say it. Are you happy?"

"No. Why would I be happy about your going to another woman, even if she is your wife?"

"You don't understand. You couldn't."

"I understand why you wouldn't want to be saddled with someone like me who can never . . ."

His grip tightened on her shoulders. "Self-pity? Stop it!" His gaze pinned her.

"It's true—"

He shook his head. "I knew when the surgery was over the chances were you'd never fully regain use of your ankle. Dyson told me, and he wanted to tell you, but I insisted that he allow you hope. Given he was a man who'd had all hope taken from him, he agreed to pray—along with me—for a miracle. There was a small chance the surgery would have prevented a permanent limp, but so small Dyson wouldn't discuss it. None of it mattered to me. I'd love you if you had no legs, Copper. The question is, will you love me once you know that I'm not the man you think I am? I'm not the Josh Redlin you know. Not even close."

She stiffened. "Obviously not." Was he a criminal on the run? A bank robber? What? At this point nothing would surprise her.

"For starters, I'm not Josh Redlin, wagon master, I'm Josh Redlin, preacher. Only problem is, I killed a man. Outright shot him, with his wife looking on."

Copper caught her breath. "Oh Josh."

"She came to me for counseling. Her husband was a mild sort, but when he was angered he turned mean. And it seems she angered him a lot. He'd caught her cheating once and nearly beat her to death. The family attended services regularly until the incident, and then he stopped coming. He stayed holed up and got more paranoid every day. She kept coming to me. I did what I could, but she had a heavy burden. God forgave her, but she couldn't forgive herself. Day after day she showed up asking that I pray with her. One day I told her I'd continue to pray with her, but she'd have to forgive herself before she could put the past behind her. We were walking down the steps of the church following one of our sessions when her husband showed up, drunk and throwing accusations. Claimed we were having an affair. When I tried to calm him he pulled a gun, threatening to blow his wife's head off."

"You were unarmed?"

"No. How I wish I had been, but I always carried a pistol. You don't live in Texas unarmed." His features tightened. "But I've wished a thousand times he'd have shot me. Instinct took over that day. When he shoved me aside and walked up to Susan and pulled his gun and aimed at her head I shot him. In the back." He paused, rubbing his hand over his chin. "I couldn't stay at the church after that. All I wanted to do was run. I knew God was aware of the circumstances, but I'd killed the father of four children and I couldn't forgive myself. I saw clearly the obstacle Susan had faced. That was five years ago. I took to leading wagon trains. I've been sending money to Susan and her kids. They've had a tough time making ends meet. She recently met a man, and they're about to be married. I went to Dallas because I knew it was unlikely I'd be back through those parts anytime soon, and I wanted to see for myself that she and the children were going to be fine." His gaze softened. "That's why I went to her first. Not out of love, but out of duty. I should have written and told you why, but I didn't much see how to put something like that in a letter."

Sweet relief flooded Copper. All this time he'd carried this burden. "Why didn't you trust me enough to tell me about Susan?"

"For the same reason you didn't trust me enough to stick around. For a long time I didn't trust anyone. Not even myself. It took a long time to work through the misery; until I met you I hadn't tried. I'd wallowed in guilt and self-pity, maybe even got a little comfortable there." He gently pulled her head to his shoulder and held her. "Until I met you, my life didn't make sense anymore. When I came back and found you were gone, I felt like I did the day I shot Susan's husband. Sick at heart."

"You could have told me sooner. I would have understood."

He eyed her. "Honey, at the time you thought I was Lucifer. If I'd told you then you'd have strung me up by my heels and let wild animals have at me."

Guilt engulfed her. How certain she had been that he wasn't trustworthy, that he didn't return her love. "But apparently you were going to let me stay in Ellsworth. You weren't coming after me?"

A smile touched the corners of his mouth. "I've been to Ellsworth—plus the fact that with Audrey and Eli's wedding coming up, I knew you'd be back any day now. I knew you wouldn't stay in that town."

She grinned as he pulled her to kiss him. They exchanged a kiss that rocked her to the core.

With lips still touching, he whispered, "So what'd you think, Miss Wilson? Think a worn-out preacher and a spitfire can marry and make a good life in Thunder Ridge?"

"If you're asking me to marry you, yes."

"I'm asking."

"I'm accepting."

She reached to touch his face, his sweet face, her face now. "Forgive me, Josh. I love you so deeply, but I forgot to trust you."

"I love you, Copper. If I admit when that love happened, I'd have to say the day I first laid eyes on you. It seems we'll have to both work on trust, but it's a learned skill." He smiled. "And we'll have the rest of our lives to acquire it."

She turned to look at the house. "You really bought this?"

He shrugged. "I knew the minute I set eyes on you I'd found the woman I want, and I knew there was no way she was going to be her happiest unless she was with her friends in Thunder Ridge."

He kissed her again with pent-up passion, and Copper knew she would never again let her doubts influence her life. If a limp was the worst this world handed her, she was truly blessed.

Easing back, he smiled. "How do you feel about being a preacher's wife?"

"But you said—"

He lightly stopped her objections with a finger to her lips. "Reverend Cordell wants to slow down. We've talked a lot this week, and he's convinced me that once a preacher, always a preacher. He's asked me to take his place, and I'd like to, Copper. I'm ready. I think we're both ready to put the past behind us, and live life fully."

Smiling, she lightly traced the outline of his face, the features she loved with all her heart and soul. She didn't have to pray about the proposal. She had perfect peace with her new future life, and God had already answered all her prayers. She'd be here in Thunder Ridge with Willow and Audrey. And Josh. Wonderful, strong Josh, the man who had shown her the meaning of sacrificial love. The words of the apostle Paul rang in her mind. *I can do all things through Christ who strengthens me.*

At that moment, Copper couldn't ask for anything more.

Dear Reader,

Thanks so much for following the very hectic lives of Willow, Audrey, and Copper. These particular characters were fun to write and hard to get out of my mind. And a very special thanks to Cynthia DiTiberio for her watchful eye and skillful editing during this series.

With every book I try to take away a personal lesson for myself. In Belles of Timber Creek the rain held significance to me. Into everyone's life, "rain" falls. While writing the series, I hit a very rough, rainy spot in my life with personal health issues and the loss of a brother, sister, and dear sister-in-law. But Willow's, Audrey's, and Copper's stories reminded me to keep my eyes up and not forward. A person can be very nearsighted when he concentrates on his efforts and not God's plans for his life. So I hope you took something lasting away with you in this series, something to hold on to when the rainy days come, because they will. But God reigns, not rains. I love that thought.

Warmly,
Lori Copeland

Discussion Questions

1. Copper went back inside a burning building to save two children, even though she had a bad ankle that hindered her from getting around very well. Do you think God gives us extra strength and courage in desperate times? Can you name a time when you received strength to face a troubled period in your life?

2. Copper and Josh had trouble trusting each other. How important is trust in a marriage?

3. The doctor wasn't there when his family needed him, but God gave him a second chance. We worship a God of second chances, so shouldn't we hand out second chances too? How quick are we to give a fallen sinner a second chance?

4. At first Copper was willing to leave the Newsomes' wagons behind. Is it all right to refuse to help someone we don't like?

5. The people in the wagon train were afraid of the Kiowa man who wanted to be with his dying mother. Is it a normal reaction to be nervous around someone who is different? How do we know when to trust? Should we trust everyone without reservation?

6. Milly was spoiled, inconsiderate, and arrogant, irritating everyone around her. How are we supposed to treat the people who irritate us?

7. Josh and Copper rode off, not knowing if the doctor would follow them. Do you believe there is a limit to what we can do for others? Does there come a time when we have to leave them alone and let them work out things for themselves? Do we sometimes use that as an excuse not to help?

8. The people in the wagon train went through some very difficult times. Sometimes as Christians we go through difficult times too, and it's easy to become discouraged. Does the Bible promise that God's people won't have trouble?

9. Copper's injury left her a cripple. For a time she felt no one would love her. In a world that stresses youth and beauty, how important are looks and outward appearances to you? Do you find yourself thinking differently about someone who is handicapped?

10. The people who were killed at the fort were victims of hatred and violence. We suffered a similar tragedy in America on September 11. How hard is it to forgive a vicious, unreasonable attack on innocent people? What should be our reaction as Christians?

11. Josh Redlin was a man of his word. How important is it that we keep our word? Is it ever all right to lie?

12. Willow, Audrey, and Copper all found true love. In a society where divorce is so common, why do you think so many marriages fail?

13. Most of us make plans for our lives. Usually those plans don't work out the way we wanted. When your plans collide with real life, can you accept it and go on, or do you become resentful, blaming God?

14. Copper tried to run away from her problems. Is it possible to run away from our troubles? Or do we take them along with us?

15. Copper and Josh are strong-willed, stubborn, and quick to say what they think. What kind of marriage do you think they'll have?

Lori Copeland

LORI COPELAND is the author of more than ninety titles, including both historical and contemporary fiction. Lori began her writing career in 1982, writing for the secular book market. In 1998, after many years of writing, Lori sensed that God was calling her to use her gift of writing to honor Him. It was at that time Lori began writing for the Christian book market.

In 2000, Lori was inducted into the Missouri Writers Hall of Fame and in 2007 was a finalist for the Christy Award. She lives in the beautiful Ozarks with her husband, Lance, their three children, and five grandchildren. Lance and Lori are very involved in their church and active in supporting mission work in Mali, West Africa.

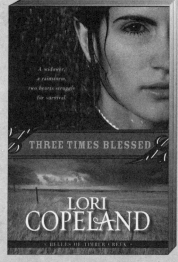